HOLIDAY RESCUE

AN ALBERTINI FAMILY ROMANCE

REBECCA ZANETTI

RAZ INK LLC

This one is for my FB street team, Rebecca's Rebels. I love you all!

ACKNOWLEDGMENTS

Thank you to everyone who helped to make this book a reality!

Thank you to Tony, Gabe, and Karlina for being an understanding and fun family who let me bounce ideas (often odd ones) off them constantly;

Thank you to Craig Zanetti, Esq. for the help with criminal law and procedure. Any mistakes about the law are mine and mine alone;

Thank you to Asha Hossain of Asha Hossain Designs, LLC for the fantastic cover;

Thank you to Debra Stewart of Dragonfly Media Ink for the wonderful edits;

Thank you to Stella Bloom for the fabulous narration for the audio book;

Thank you to Liz Berry, Jillian Stein, Asa Maria Bradley, and Boone Brux for the advice with the concepts for this new series;

Thank you to my incredibly hard working agent, Caitlin Blasdell;

Thank you to Sara and Gwen from Fresh Fiction, and Cissy and crew from WriterSpace for helping get the word out about this new series;

Thank you to my fantastic assistant, Anissa Beatty, for all of the excellent work and for being such a great leader for Rebecca's Rebels (my FB street team);

Thank you to FB Rebel Amanda Singletary for her creativity with helping to name this novella, and thank you to Rebel Kimberly Detillier Rogers for coming up with a series name if I bundle the novellas;

Thank you to Rebels Heather Frost, Karen Clemente, Karen Fisher, and Kimberly Frost for being proof-reading angels;

Thank you to my constant support system: Gail and Jim English, Kathy and Herbie Zanetti, Debbie and Travis Smith, Stephanie and Don West, and Jessica and Jonah Namson.

NOTE FROM THE AUTHOR

Howdy everyone! Thank you for so much support for his new series of mine. Sometimes, as an author, you have to write something a little different. This series is that for me.

I've loved the emails and FB notes about this series, and I'm happy to keep writing about Anna and her family. Sometimes we need a little bit of humor, right? This is a side note for the family with a full romance, which was fun to write.

Also, I am a lawyer, and I might live in a small town, but this is in **no way** autobiographical. It turns out that the name Albertini is a distant family name of my relatives, which is pretty cool. However, the story is all made up. The characters are all fictional and so are the towns and counties (like usual). Also, the law is correct. :)

I hope you like Anna's world as much as I do!

Also, to stay up to date with releases, free content, and tons of contests, follow me on Bookbub, Facebook, the FB Rebel Street Team, and definitely subscribe to my newsletter for FREE BOOKS!

Also, I like to pair up with other bestselling authors to cross promote and give away books in our newsletters, so I will be giving away copies of my friends' books coming up. Just go to my website (RebeccaZanetti.com) to sign up for my newsletter.

XO

Rebecca

CHAPTER 1

A wet nose touched Heather's, and she opened her eyes to see the prettiest brown eyes imaginable. Large and soft with a sparkle of puppy adoration and triumph in them. The dog licked her chin, sat on its haunches, and barked three times.

Heather blinked freezing snow out of her eyes and sat up straighter against the solid tree trunk, trying to get her bearings. Her butt and legs were chilled from the frozen ground. She must've drifted off beneath the sweeping pine boughs after pressing her personal locator beacon for help.

Pain ticked through her head, and she gingerly tried to move her injured ankle, biting her lip at the agony. That's right. She looked over her shoulder at the rocky and icy terrain she'd fallen down after slipping on the trail near the top of the mountain. Her pack was next to her, and she patted it, wincing as wet snow splashed up. Then she focused on the quietly panting Black Labrador. "Hello."

The dog's tail wagged across the snowy pine needles. It wore a bright red Search and Rescue vest along with a wide collar with a box that had a blinking red light. Heather had fallen into some sort of gulley, surrounded by trees with one very rocky edge

1

heading back up to the main trail. The rocks were black slate, icy, and sharp.

A whistle sounded from up above, and the dog barked three more times before laying down with its nose on its paws right in front of Heather. Snow scattered.

"Good girl, Zena," came a masculine voice. "Hello? Can you hear me?"

Heather angled around the tree and tried to look up and beyond the jagged rocks. "I can hear you."

"What are your injuries?" The man was tall against the rapidly darkening sky, and his face remained in shadow.

Heather swallowed. "A few bruises and I think a broken ankle." There was no 'think' about it. "It's broken for sure," she yelled, trying not to shiver. Was she going into shock?

"All right. Two of us are coming down, so stay behind that tree in case we loosen rocks or ice," he called down, his tone remaining calm.

"Okay," she chirped. Then she hunkered down behind the tree. Oh, she'd definitely expected danger to come her way, but not out by herself scattering her grandma's ashes on the mountain top. She'd worry about her disastrous life later. For now, she studied the rescue dog, which had the loveliest black coat she'd ever seen. "Zena, huh? You do look like a warrior princess."

The dog kept perfectly still, watching her as if she didn't want her prize to wander away. Her brown eyes were alert and smart, and she vibrated as the rescuers maneuvered down the large rocks toward them. Her training was as impressive as her obvious intelligence. Snow landed on her nose.

Heather listened as sure steps made their way down the craggy rocks, and soon a man stood before her. She'd been wrong. *He* had the prettiest eyes she'd ever seen. They were a tawny brown, lighter in the middle of the iris, the color spiking out into deep chocolate rims. "Hi." He dropped to his haunches to study her face.

Maybe she was still unconscious because no way was this guy real. Dark and mussed-up hair swept away from a rugged face with more than a couple days of whiskers across his edged jaw. His chest was broad, his hands wide, and his gaze intent. "Hi," she whispered.

The dog perked up and moved to the man's side, tail still wagging.

He patted the dog's neck. "You've already met Zena, and I'm Quint Albertini. Want to tell me what happened?"

Albertini? Yeah, he looked Italian. "I was hiking down the trail and slipped." Then she'd tumbled over the rocks, bruising herself, until landing next to the tree. "I think my ankle is broken."

He reached for a flashlight in his pack and shone it at her foot, which she'd already wrapped before putting a warmer at her toes and struggling to wear another sock over it all. "Looks like a solid wrap." He looked at her hiking boot, which was near her pack. "Good idea taking the boot off before the ankle got too swollen."

Another man jumped from a rock and landed. This guy was also in his late twenties, maybe early thirties, and had dark brown hair and strong features. Like Quint, he wore hiking clothing, a red Search and Rescue vest, and a backpack. "What do we have?"

"Broken ankle," Quint confirmed. "Her eyes are clear and I don't see signs of a concussion." He leaned toward her. "Are you hurt anywhere else?"

"Just bruised," she admitted. "I'd walk but can't put any weight on the ankle." There was no way to hop back up the rocky embankment to the trail.

Quint looked over his shoulder. "This is Rory, my brother."

"Hi. I'm Heather," she said, the cold starting to get to her. She shivered.

Rory grinned. "Great job taking the PLB with you. Most hikers aren't that careful."

"I was hiking alone," she said. "So I figured having a personal locator beacon was just smart." She'd hit the panic button the second she'd landed and regained her pack.

Quint looked closer at her ankle. "As well as boot warmers, extra socks, and granola bars?" The remains of a wrapper stuck out of a pocket of the backpack.

"I like to be prepared," she murmured, trying not to feel like a dork.

The wind sped up and splashed water off boughs toward them.

Rory peered up at the bruised looking clouds. "I know we've had a really late and light winter, but hiking Storm's Peak in December is a bad idea. There's another storm moving in, and we need to get going." He reached for a radio and told somebody that they'd found the hiker. Then he paused. "Do we need the litter?"

She knew from her research that a litter was the stretcher rescuers used to carry an injured person down a mountain. While December wasn't a good month to hike, she'd had to wait to get the permits for her grandmother's ashes, and it had looked like the storm would hold off for another couple of days. The local weather forecast had been incorrect.

Quint looked her over, and her body somehow warmed. "I'd prefer not to use the litter. The terrain is too rocky and slick." He leaned in. "In cases like this, it's a lot easier to piggy you out. Are you up to it?"

Her eyebrows rose. "You want to give me a piggyback?"

Rory chuckled. "It is the easiest way, and we do it all the time. The question is if you can hold on."

"I think you're going into shock," Quint said, eyeing her snowy and wet jacket.

She could handle this. "I'm okay. I can hold on."

"Good." His gaze lightened. "It'll be a lot easier to climb up these boulders if you're on my back."

She breathed out and tried to sound cool and not like a love struck teenager. He was going to carry her out? Flutters wandered through her abdomen. "All right. Let me take off my other boot."

He held up a hand. "You can keep it on."

"No." She tried to sit up straighter. "It'll be easier for me to balance with both boots off, and that way, I won't keep kicking you." She winced. "I'll apologize now for the late season huckleberry milkshakes I've been eating all week. I'm sure I was five pounds lighter last Monday."

His smile warmed her enough to push the sense of shock away.

* * *

QUINT KEPT a watch on the woman's focus and complexion. Her eyes were clear but her mouth pinched with pain. She was pale but definitely putting on a brave face. Her eyes were the light green of his Nonna's antique glassware and her hair a natural sandy blonde, and even beneath the snow gear, he could tell she had curves. A lot of curves.

He was a man who appreciated curves.

For now, he had to ignore her obvious allure and get her off this mountain before the next storm tried to take them out. It was a late winter, but they were about to be bombarded with snow. Thunder bellowed in the distance, promising rain first, and she jumped.

"It's okay," he said, turning his attention back to her ankle. "Your wrap is good, but I'm worried my movements will impact the ankle and really hurt you." They could put her on the litter and lift her via ropes, but time wasn't on their side. Carrying her out would be so much faster.

She gulped. "If I hold tight with my thighs, it'll keep my ankle still. I can do it." She glanced at the threatening sky, and her lips trembled.

That was not sexual. He mentally slapped himself in the head. Her scent of apple cider and cinnamon was going to drive him crazy, and he needed to get a grip on himself. He had a job to do.

Rory peered over his shoulder. "Your jacket will make it difficult for her to hold on, but she's wet. Thoughts?"

Quint stayed on his haunches. "Heather? How do you feel about being inside my jacket? It'll give you stability and I'll keep you warm, but you'll need to take off your wet coat." He had to prevent her from going into shock, but he wanted to give her all the sense of control he could. The woman had to be terrified, even though she was trying to hide it.

"That works," she said, her hands pressing the ground so she could stand.

"Whoa," he said. "I'll help you." He held out his hands, and when she tentatively took them, he stood and gently lifted her with him. Her skin was soft and her wrist bones fragile.

She kept her weight on one foot with the injured ankle lifted. "You're tall."

He grinned. "So they tell me. You're not." He was about a foot or so taller than her at six-foot-two.

Her smile was pained. "I've heard."

"All right." He kept her hands. "Rory is going to help you with your coat while I assist with your balance. Don't worry. He's very rarely a pervert."

Rory moved in. "Our mama would kick my butt if I even thought of being a pervert. That woman has been practicing Kenpo, too. She could probably do some damage." His voice was cheerful and reassuring as he unzipped the jacket to reveal Heather's plain white T-shirt and then removed the coat.

She looked down at her wet and slick pants. "I have leggings on beneath these."

Rory folded her jacket and set it in her backpack. "I can help."

She hesitated. "I, ah, feel like we've all bonded here and can keep a secret or two." Her pretty face blushed, and a dusting of snow landed on her head.

Quint paused. "All right?" Curiosity grabbed him around the neck.

She sighed. "The leggings are my favorite, but I'd never wear them in public."

Rory chuckled. "It's okay. We all have pants with holes in them."

She shook her head and looked down. "No. No holes. It's just, they're so comfortable. But they have...BABYCAKES across the butt."

Amusement smacked into Quint. God, she was adorable. "We won't tell a soul."

She looked up, humor and pain still reflected in those unreal eyes. "Seriously. They were black, and I've washed them so many times that they're a soft gray color now, except the letters are still bright pink. It's like magic."

Rory laughed out loud. "We have definitely bonded and will keep your dastardly secret. Let's do this."

"I can." She released Quint's hands and reached for the waist of her rain pants.

Quint grasped her shoulders to help her balance and protect the broken ankle. She pushed down the slickers to reveal very nice and form-fitting leggings that were, indeed, a well washed gray color. He helped her step out of them and then released her before shrugging off his jacket. "Rory?" He turned around.

"Yep." Rory moved toward the woman. "Heather, you reach for his shoulders and I'll lift. Okay?"

"Okay," she gasped.

Quint leaned down so she could reach his shoulders, and Rory lifted her onto his back. She gave a slight hiss of pain, and then her thighs clamped against his ribs. Rory took the jacket and helped Quint with one arm, set the material around them both, and then did the other arm before zipping it up.

The woman felt solid and cold against Quint's back. "You'll warm up soon. How's the ankle?"

"Okay," she whispered against his neck. "I think my arms

7

should go under?" She moved her hands from his shoulders to beneath his arms, flattening them on his chest.

"Yeah," he said, checking his balance. "If your shoulders start to ache, you can put your arms over my neck, but wait until we get to the top of this cliff, okay?"

"Okay." She turned her head into his neck and snuggled, her body going soft and relaxed against him.

The trust blasted through his heart, and he took a moment. "You're safe, Heather. I'm not going to let anything happen to you." Her life was now in his hands, and as far as he was concerned, she'd never been safer. "Zena is going to lead the way up, you and I will follow her, and Rory will bring up the rear with the packs. You ready?"

"Yes," she said softly. "Um, Quint?"

"Yeah?" He turned on his hat headlamp and scouted the best way up the rocks.

She cleared her throat. "I was a little cold and scared. I might cry a mite now that I'm safe." A tear slid against his bare neck.

That easily, she slipped right into his heart, where she couldn't be. He had enough problems right now. Even so, for the moment, she was his responsibility. He started hiking up the dangerous and rocky embankment as the snow began to beat the freezing rain down. "Cry all you want, sweetheart. I've got you."

CHAPTER 2

*H*eather rested in the hospital bed with her broken ankle elevated. Someone had decorated the room with poinsettias, and soft Christmas music wound through the hallway outside. She frowned at the offending cast that protected what had turned out to be a clean break. At least that was something. She needed to be in fighting form, just in case, and running with crutches was an impossibility.

Her mind returned—again—to the handsome rescuer who'd carried her up the rocky cliff and down the mountain in what had turned into a blinding snowstorm. Quint Albertini. He was sexy and strong, and right now, she wanted to snuggle right back into his neck.

That was not going to happen.

She sighed and looked around the quiet hospital room where she'd stayed the remainder of the night. There was no reason to still be in bed, but the nurse hadn't returned with her discharge papers yet.

A bustle sounded outside the doorway, and a woman strode inside. She was tall with gray streaked black hair piled on her head and smooth skin with sparkling brown eyes. Quint's eyes.

The woman looked a little bit like Sophia Loren, and her red Christmas sweater appeared classy instead of silly.

"Hello." She pulled a pink chair closer to the bed and handed over a platter of cookies to place on the blanket. "I brought you goodies. The food in the Silverville hospital isn't bad, but nothing tastes as good as iced Christmas cookies."

The fragrant smell made Heather's nose twitch. "Um, thank you?" She reached for a cookie. It was only the second day of December, and the lady already had Christmas cookies?

Was the woman the small town's version of a Candy Striper? Heather took a bite and then had to take a moment. Warmth, almond, and sugar hit her system with a sense of love. Chewing, she swallowed. "This is the best cookie I've tasted in my entire life."

The woman smiled. "Of course it is. It's an old Italian recipe."

"Of course," Heather murmured, taking another bite. So good. "I'm Heather."

"I know, dear. You're Louise Davis's granddaughter, right? I was so sorry to hear of her passing, even though she just moved here last month." The woman reached over and patted Heather's hand. "I'm Elda Albertini."

Albertini. "You're Quint's mom? He saved me last night." Heather eyed the cookie plate.

Elda pushed the plate closer. "Aren't you a sweet girl? I'm Quintino's *grandmother*. My second eldest son is Quint's father. Everyone calls me Nonna Albertini."

Grandmother? Whatever the woman's skincare regimen was, Heather wanted to learn it. "It's so very nice to meet you. Grams sent me a letter saying how nice everyone was in town, and I was looking forward to visiting and meeting everyone." Before Grams had died unexpectedly from a stroke. Sadness wandered through Heather, and she reached for a second cookie. Why not?

Elda patted her hand again. "I didn't have the time to get to know your grandmother, but she seemed lovely. Do you have any other family?"

"No," Heather said, the sense of feeling alone swamping her. She shoved it away. "It was just Grams and me for most of my life. We lived in Boise until recently when Grams moved up here to fully retire." It had been a month since she'd passed, and Heather was still grieving, but the good memories helped. "She was the best person in the world." She tried to sit up straighter in the bed. "Her last wish was to have her ashes scattered into the wind from the top of Storm Mountain, and it took me a couple of weeks to get the right permits. That's why I was up there in the winter. I was hoping to miss the snowstorm."

"That was the right thing to do," Elda said, nodding emphatically. "It's going to be a late and wild winter season if my arthritic aching hands are anything to go by, and they are. You should stay off the mountain until next spring unless you're in a four-wheeler or on a snowmobile. No hiking."

"I agree." Heather looked down at her cast and sighed.

Elda reached for a cookie and munched contentedly. "You said that you lived in Boise. Past tense."

Heather nodded. "I did, but Grams left me her house, so I'm moving here. I can work from anywhere, and the town is so sweet and quaint." More importantly, it didn't have the bane of her existence living there. It was safe and strangers were noticed.

"That's wonderful." Elda finished her cookie and smiled. "What do you do?"

"I write and illustrate children's books." Heather perked up. "In fact, I'd love to start a new series featuring a rescue dog now that I've met Zena." The ideas were already spinning around in her head.

Elda's eyes sparkled. "Then you must get to know Zena better, right? We have a family barbecue every Sunday at my eldest son's house, and I'll give you directions."

Heather's mouth opened and then shut. "That's kind of you, but I would never want to impose."

"Don't be silly." Elda opened a flower decorated purse and rummaged around to bring out a pen and a small notepad. "Your grandma told me that your great uncle on her father's side was Italian. A Banerosi, I believe."

Heather blinked. "That sounds right."

Elda quickly jotted down an address and handed the paper over. "Isn't that wonderful?"

"Sure?" Heather was saved from having to find a more appropriate answer when Quint strode inside with Zena bounding beside him. Her body warmed and heat flushed into her face. "Hello."

"Hi." In the daylight, he was even more handsome. His dark hair curled beneath his ears, and his eyes were a light topaz today. He'd shaved, but a shadow was already covering what had to be considered a truly rugged jaw. Today he wore jeans and a faded tee that hugged very firm chest muscles Heather had felt the night before while he hiked down a mountain during a snowstorm and saved her life. He looked at his grandmother. "Nonna?"

"Hi, sweetheart." Elda patted Zena on the head and then stood to reach up and place a kiss on his chin. "I was just talking to Heather, and she has Italian ancestry. Isn't that just lovely?"

Quint sighed. "Nonna."

Elda turned and smiled at Heather. "She was just telling me what a hero you are and how you saved her. At least you didn't drop *her*." With that, she patted Zena again and strode toward the door.

"That was eons ago." Quint rolled his eyes. "I didn't drop Anna, Nonna. Donna and I were swinging her and threw her in the river."

"She broke her wrist," Elda said smoothly.

"It was nearly two decades ago. She was four years old and she landed on a board that we didn't know was floating in the water."

Quint shrugged his powerful shoulders. "I still maintain it wasn't our fault, and Anna doesn't hold any grudges. Well, until she wants a favor."

"That's between you and your cousin." Elda waved from the doorway. "Heather is coming to the Sunday barbecue, and she probably shouldn't drive. Take care of it." Then she was gone.

Quint dropped into her vacated chair, his gaze direct on Heather. "Unless you want to get married next week, you're gonna want to run. Trust me."

Heather's mouth went dry. "Um."

He grinned, his muscled body overwhelming the simple chair. "You were probably somewhat safe until she discovered you have Italian blood. Now you're fair game, so be prepared for match-making as you've never seen before."

She barely knew the man, but a sense of peace and comforta-bility surrounded her—along with intrigue. "I figured you'd be married."

"Nope. Have terrible luck with women." His broad hand descended on the dog's head. "Except for my girl, here."

"I know what you mean," Heather admitted, instantly shying away from the possibility. She had enough problems right now, although hopefully moving to the small Idaho town would take care of most of them. "I do want to thank you for carrying me down the mountain."

"Any time." He pet the dog, whose tail wagged across the sparkling clean tiled floor. "Mind if I ask what you were doing hiking that mountain in the beginning of December?"

"I was scattering my grandmother's ashes," she murmured. "It took forever to get the permits."

Understanding smoothed out his features. "I'm sorry about that."

So was she. Heather pushed the plate of cookies toward him. "Hungry?"

"Definitely." He took a cookie and ate happily. "She makes the best ones, right?"

Heather could only nod. Pleasure cut across his angled face, and man, he was something to look at and probably draw later. "Do you carry a lot of people down mountains?"

"Enough," he said agreeably. "The Silverville Search and Rescue team gets a good workout pretty often, and we coordinate with the state and federal officials when necessary. We're all volunteers, but most of us grew up around here and know the terrain."

Volunteers? She looked at the dog. "What do you do when you're not volunteering and putting yourself in danger?"

He snagged another cookie. "I'm a Forestry Technician with the U.S. Forest Service."

That made sense. He seemed like an outdoorsy type of guy, and managing the forests was a good job. A solid job in a place like Idaho. "It's nice you're stationed at home," she said.

"Well, I live here but have to travel for work quite a bit," he admitted. "Although with my schedule, I do get some great downtime, and usually being with family is a good thing." He set his hands in his lap, even though his gaze dropped to the cookies.

"Please, have another one," she said. "I already ate two, and that's my sugar limit for the day." Or close to it, anyway.

He shrugged and took another cookie.

"Who's Anna?" She couldn't help but ask.

"My cousin," Quint said, wiping icing off his lip with his thumb. "We were playing and having fun. Her older sister and I were swinging her toward the river, I had her arms, and Donna had her feet, and we tossed, and she hit a board. Two decades ago." He shook his head. "But when Nonna wants something, she's more than happy to use guilt, you know? I mean, Donna and I were about eight years old, and Anna asked us to throw her in. We were goofing off, and Anna rarely brings it up."

The fondness with which he spoke caught Heather in the

chest. What would it be like to have a big family with so much history? So much support and love? "You're very lucky," she whispered.

"I know," he said, his gaze warming on her. "Don't worry. Now that you're in Silverville, you're family. Whether you want to be or not." His chuckle was low and throaty to the point of being sexy.

Her phone buzzed from her pack, which sat on the granite counter, and she stiffened.

He tilted his head. "Want me to get that?"

"No. That's okay. I'll call them back," she said, her heart rate kicking up.

"You sure?" His humor had gone, leaving a curious and rather intense look in his eyes.

She waved the stress away. "Of course." She could handle it. "It's probably just my editor, and I'll call her back later." Hopefully it was Julie.

"All right." He scratched Zena behind the ears, his gaze no less intense.

Heels clip-clopped closer in the hallway outside, and a woman stepped inside. She had blonde hair, blue eyes, and bright red nails. "Quint," she said, her very red lips tipping in a smile. "Hello."

Quint frowned. "What are you doing here?"

So much for the good natured forestry guy. Heather studied the woman. Her skirt was tight and short, her blouse Chanel, and her earrings real diamonds. Her body was small and looked perfect in the tight skirt, and Heather made sure the blankets were covering her much larger legs...except for the cast.

"Hi. I'm Jolene." The woman ignored Quint and walked closer, her gaze raking Heather. "I'm from the *Timber Gazette*, and I'd like to interview you for a feature about your ordeal. We have a local imprint for the paper here in Silverville. What do you say?"

Fear shot straight to Heather's stomach and cramped. Hard. "I'd rather not," she said, aiming for forceful but coming out unsure. Her throat began to close, and she fought off panic. "I mean, thank you for your interest, but I don't want an interview." She looked at Quint. "I'm sorry. I'm sure it'd help the volunteer program, but…." She couldn't really explain.

"No problem." He stood and put his body between Jolene and Heather. "She said no. That means no." His voice was firm with a hint of something beneath. Irritation? Anger?

Jolene's hand wrapped around his wrist, the red nails looking sharp. "Now, Quint. Knock it off. I was hoping we could grab a drink and talk things out, anyway."

Heather's heart twinged, even though there was no reason she should think about romance right now. Even so, if this was the type Quint liked, there hadn't been a shot in hell, anyway. The woman was high-end designer store, and Heather was more of a Target girl in the bigger sizes.

Nope. *Bad self-talk*. She mentally shook herself out of it. For goodness sakes.

Quint removed the woman's hand. "Sorry, I can't. I promised Heather a ride home, and here comes Nurse O'Connor with the discharge papers."

A ride home?

CHAPTER 3

Quint parked in front of Heather's house and jumped out of his truck to reach the passenger side door before she could open it. Her place was ready for the holidays. Christmas lights were already strewn across the eaves, and a decorated tree stood front and center in the bay window. "Let me. I'm getting used to carrying you."

She blushed. "You're just trying to build more muscle."

He laughed and lifted her out, figuring she'd just given permission. Seeing her attempt walking with the crutches to his truck earlier had been painful. "You are a good sport, Heather." In fact, she hadn't even asked about the weird interaction with Jolene. Yet, anyway. He let Zena leap out and then shut the door. "I'll come back for your stuff. Let's get you out of the snow." The storm had lightened but wasn't letting go yet.

She ducked her head against the blizzard but kept silent.

He hustled up the walk to the front porch of the old Denzi place. It was an A-frame home with two bedrooms, one bathroom, and climbable trees in the back that led to the national forest. "My friend Joe lived here with his folks while growing up. Both of them are gone, and Joe is a cop in New York City." He set her down beneath the eve and by the front door, turning the knob. It was locked. "Huh. Never saw it locked before." But it made sense. The world had changed, and Heather was a woman living alone. "Key?"

"In my pack," she said, hopping on her good foot to lean against the freshly painted white siding. The shutters had been painted a muted blue that looked pretty in the winter light.

Zena ran around back to the fully grown pine trees, barking happily while playing in the snow.

"No problem." Quint loped down the steps to his truck to grab her pack and crutches, returning to unlock the door and help her inside. He whistled. "Wow. This place looks great." The genuine wooden floors had been refinished, the walls painted, and new granite showed through the doorway to the kitchen. The house had been built in the early 1900s when the mines were prosperous, and the craftsmanship was obvious with the vintage high ceilings. However, boxes were strewn in every direction.

"They remodeled before my grandmother bought the place." Heather leaned on the crutches and looked around, her shoulders slumping. "She didn't have time to fully unpack, and the rest of the stuff here is mine. It might take me longer than I'd hoped." She shook her head and smiled. "But it's not like I could go hiking or running right now."

Everything inside him wanted to help, but Heather was a keeper, and he wasn't at a place in his life for a keeper. Not with his job and definitely not with his recent run of bad decisions, including Jolene. "The tree is, ah, interesting." The tree was green but every decoration was pink. Pink Santas, pink picture frames, pink ornaments with brighter pink accents. "I take it your grandma liked pink?"

Heather laughed and nodded. Man, she had a great laugh.

A small compact car skidded to a stop on the street, and Quint turned to look with the door still open. The youngest McLeary kid leaped out of the car wearing a bright red hat with a pizza box in his hands. He ran through the snow to reach them.

Quint sighed. "Hey, Smash. Great game the other night."

"Hey, Quint. Thanks." The kid shoved the pizza box into his hands. "It's already paid for and she tipped me. Bye." He nodded at Heather and then headed back for his car.

Heather stared at the box and frowned. "I didn't order pizza."

"No. I'm sure it's from Nonna Albertini." Quint strode into the fresh kitchen and placed the box on the island. "I'm sorry about this. She's a born matchmaker, and she's determined."

Heather wobbled behind him on the crutches. "Oh." A peach color filtered through her high cheekbones. "Well, would you like to stay for an early dinner? It's the least I can do, considering you saved my life and your grandmother bought the pizza." Humor danced across her face.

He looked toward the doorway.

"Oh. Zena can come inside." Heather hobbled to the cupboards and took down some Appleware dishes. "I have a bottle of Cabernet over by the microwave."

"That sounds good." Still, he hesitated. "I just don't—"

She turned and hit him full on with those light green eyes. "I don't, either. Believe me. While I like your Nonna a lot, and she bakes the most incredible cookies in the world, I'm not looking for romance. At all. Now isn't a good time."

Should he be insulted? Yeah, it was exactly what he'd planned to say, but still. He had carried the woman down a fucking mountain. But he should be glad they were on the same page and needed to check his ego where it belonged. "All right. Friends?" he asked.

"Yeah. Friends," she said, her voice softer than those pretty eyes. Both punched him right below the belt. Figuratively.

He whistled, and Zena bounded around the porch and lurched inside, sliding into a box. She fell back onto her butt and then panted, her tail wagging across the wooden floor. "Down girl," he murmured.

She flopped down, sighed, and put her nose on her paws.

Heather chuckled. "She is so well trained."

"She'd better be," he allowed. They trained all the time, so the canine had better behave. Not that he didn't adore her, and she knew it. After rescuing Heather the night before, he'd played with the dog as a reward for an hour before making them both go to sleep.

Heather's phone buzzed from her backpack, and he reached in without thinking and turned to hand it to her. She'd gone pale.

He paused. "You okay?"

"Yeah." She visibly shook herself out of it. "Seriously. I'm fine." She reached for the phone, glanced at the screen, and frowned.

"Does an 'unknown caller' concern you?" he asked. Yeah, he'd taken a look at the screen.

Her laugh was off key, and her hands shaky. "No. I'm sure it's just a telemarketer. It's a new number, so almost nobody knows it." She clicked the phone off. "So. Pizza?"

"Sure." His mind was already ticking. Who was she afraid of?

* * *

HEATHER PATTED her stomach after eating truly delicious pizza. Her brain was a little fuzzy from the wine, but her ankle no longer hurt, so there was a bright side. "Make sure you thank your grandmother for the pizza." She couldn't help but stare a little at Quint across the table. In the soft light as the storm strengthened outside, he looked large and formidable in her kitchen. Strong and protective. "Quintino."

He grinned. "She tried to call me Tino when I was younger, and my dad quickly nicknamed me Quint."

"Do you have siblings?" she asked.

"Yeah. I have five brothers." He reached and poured them both more wine. "I also have many, many, many cousins, and we're all close."

She sipped the rich Cabernet and let the warmth spread throughout her body. "Like Anna and Donna."

"Yes," he said, taking another drink.

"Are those Italian names?" Not that it mattered, but now her curiosity had arisen.

He chuckled, and the sound wandered along her nerve endings, electrifying the sensation. "Yes and no. Their dad married a full-on Irish woman, and the compromise was that each of the girls got an Irish and an Italian name. So we have Donatella Tiffany, Contessa Carmelina, and Annabella Fiona Albertini in that family. We're all close, and I'm sure you'll meet them if you stay in town."

How freaking charming. She loved that story. How she wished she had cousins like that. "They live here?"

"No. All three live over the pass in Timber City, but they come home a lot."

Timber City was about fifty minutes through a mountain pass, and Heather had already headed over to do some shopping. It was a quaint touristy type town with lakes, rivers, and many golf courses, from what she'd seen. "I take it they attend this already famous family barbecue every Sunday?"

"They'd better," he said, his grin boyish. "How can Nonna work on matchmaking them if they're never around? She's been on a tear with Tessa lately, and I think it's because Anna put her up to it, but I can't prove that fact. It has been nice for her to concentrate on poor Tessa and Nick Basanelli and leave me alone for a while."

Speaking of which. Heather had no right to ask. "What about Jolene?" Yeah, she'd asked. Must be the wine taking effect.

Quint sighed. "Jolene was a mistake. Way back when, she was older in high school, and I didn't really know her. This August, I returned home from a job that was pretty rough. I got home, got drunk, and ended up in Jolene's bed." He held up a hand. "Not an excuse, I know. But then she wanted to date, and we went on a few dates, and then I found out she was dogging Anna and writing crappy articles for the paper about my cousins. So I ended it."

"Were the articles factual?" Heather took another drink of the deep wine.

"Maybe factual but with a definite slant that made Anna and Donna look bad," he said. "Jolene has a mean streak, and I didn't know about it until they found out I was dating her." He grimaced. "They made sure I knew it all, and I still gave her the benefit of the doubt, which she exploited." He finished his drink, and his masculine neck moved as he swallowed. "We all make mistakes, and that was mine for the decade."

Her phone buzzed, and she reached for it from the counter. It was another unknown caller. It had to be a telemarketer.

"Why don't you answer it?" Quint asked, his body still.

Yeah. Why didn't she? There was no way Jack had tracked down her new number. "Hello?"

"Hello, gorgeous. How's northern Idaho?" Jack asked.

Panic ricocheted throughout her extremities, and her fingers and toes tingled with the anxiety. "You have the wrong number," she said, ending the call. Then she looked up at Quint while putting the phone aside. Her ears rang. "Darn telemarketers." Her voice came out hoarse. How had he found her so quickly? She'd only had the new number for two weeks.

"You okay?" Quint's voice sounded like he came from far away.

"Of course." She reached for her glass and downed the rest of the contents in three large gulps. "I'm fine." She put the glass gently on the table.

He cocked his head, and that dark gaze bore right through her. "Uh huh. How about you tell me what's going on? I can be a great sounding board."

She blinked and forced a smile. "Nothing is going on." The man had saved her enough for this lifetime, especially since he'd already put her into the friend zone. Of course, she'd put him there, too. Mainly because her life was a disaster, and he apparently liked sporty looking blondes with mean streaks, and she so did not fit that bill. "While I'm sure you're accustomed to helping your cousins with problems, I'm a big girl and can handle mine."

"So you admit you have a problem," he drawled.

She faltered. "No. If I did, I could handle it."

"Honey, all of my cousins can handle their own problems and normally do, especially since half the time, they create the problems. However, we're all smart enough to ask for help when we need it. Right now, you're shaky, pale, and look like you're about to bolt." He glanced at the crutches leaning against the wall. "Or hobble. Either way, who was on the phone?"

"Nobody," she lied. So Jack knew she had a new number, but the state was big, so he probably didn't know where exactly she was living. The wind threw ice against the windows, and she jumped.

Quint stood and threw all the garbage away before taking the empty wine glasses to rinse out in the sink. His broad shoulders tapered down to a narrow waist. "I can help."

"You already have," she said honestly, trying really hard not to look at his hard butt. Nope. Failed. He had a spectacular behind. She cleared her throat. "I appreciate everything you've done, and again, thank you for the pizza. Or thank your grandmother."

He turned around to face her. "I will. Or you can thank her yourself at the Sunday barbecue. I'll pick you up at three in the afternoon." With that, he headed toward her door.

She stood. Barbecue? Had she accepted the invitation? The more time she spent with Quint Albertini, the more she wanted to break free from the friend zone. Big time. It was Friday, and getting over this silly crush she had on him in a day wasn't likely. "That's probably not a good idea."

His chuckle as he opened her front door didn't help. "No kidding. Lock your door." With that, he and Zena left her alone in her quiet, messy, solid house. She hopped to the door and locked it, peeking out the side window as they jumped into his truck.

Yep. Quint had a truly excellent ass. But she had enough to worry about.

Her phone buzzed again from the kitchen.

CHAPTER 4

*T*he snow finally let up around midmorning on Saturday, and Heather sat on her floor emptying boxes, enjoying the moment as sunlight poked through the clouds outside and made the room brighter. Christmas music played from the kitchen, and she hummed along, trying to calm her nerves. Jack had kept calling until she'd just turned off the phone the night before.

A knock sounded on her door, and she yelped. "Um, just a second." It couldn't be him. She needed to get a gun. Wasn't it legal to carry anywhere in Idaho? What was the law? She pushed to her foot and hopped toward the door, looking through the side window at three women on her front porch. Were they selling something? She opened the door. "Hello."

"Hi." The first woman was about five-four with rich brown hair and sparkling grayish-green eyes. "I'm Anna." She slid a heated latte into Heather's hand and walked inside, looking around. "This place looks awesome. Check out what they did with the floors." Then she moved toward the kitchen. "Oh, the granite is exquisite."

The next woman had dark hair, brown eyes and looked a lot

like Quint. "Excuse my sister. She's usually falling out of trees or getting arrested and isn't housebroken yet. I'm Donna." Donna held out a hand, and Heather took it to shake.

"I'm Tessa." The third woman moved inside and looked around. She had reddish-blonde hair, green eyes, and adorable freckles. "Quint sent us." She carried a box toward the kitchen. "I brought donuts from Smiley's Diner in Timber City where I work. I didn't know what kind you liked, so I brought an assortment." Her voice carried as she moved.

Donna smiled. "Give in now. We're here to drink coffee, eat donuts, and help you unpack. You have a broken ankle, and it'll take forever without help."

Heather hopped with her latte to the kitchen. "This is really kind of you, but I've got it under control."

Anna flipped open the donut box on the island. "Plates?"

Heather pointed to the cupboard.

Tessa opened it to bring out Appleware. "I love this pattern. We have it in our family, too." She put four salad plates on the island. "What kind do you like?"

Heather's head spun. "Um, chocolate?" She liked all donuts, really.

"Here you go." Anna tossed a chocolate donut on a plate and then put a maple bar on another plate to hand to Tessa. "Donna, do you want maple or sugar-glazed?" she called.

"Don't care," Donna said from the living room. "I forgot how tall these ceilings were. The place is so roomy."

Anna put a maple bar on a plate and then took one with sprinkles for herself. "How's the ankle?"

Heather ate a bite of the fresh donut. If she kept hanging out with the Albertinis, she'd need to buy new clothes. "It's okay. I find that hopping is easier than using crutches."

Anna ate her donut. "Yeah. I hurt my ankle earlier this summer, and hopping was definitely the way to go."

"After falling out of a tree," Donna said quietly against her latte, her lips twitching.

Anna rolled her eyes. "I was being chased by a couple of guys with guns. It happens."

Heather paused. What in the world?

Anna waved the unspoken question away. "Long story. I'm a lawyer."

Did that explain guys with guns and trees? Perhaps for the Albertini family, it did. "Listen. I really appreciate you coming, and it was nice of Quint to call you, but you must all be busy with your own lives." Running from guys with guns at the very least. Although, the idea that Quint had tried to provide her with assistance warmed her in inappropriate places, and she had to knock that off right now.

Tessa reached for a partially unpackaged box on the small table in the kitchen nook. "It's either us or our mom, Quint's mom, and probably Nonna. You'll be engaged by sundown in that case."

Heather gulped.

"Sundown?" Anna sputtered. "What are you, in a western now?"

Tessa grinned. "I've been watching *Longmire* on Netflix. That Bailey Chase is a hottie. He plays Branch." She pulled out a bowl made of pink depression glassware. "Oh, this is beautiful."

Heather nodded. "I found it in an antique store near Sun Valley. We don't have many family heirlooms or collections or anything like that, so I figured I'd start one, you know? I like the pink, green, and watermelon depression glassware." It was classic and beautiful.

Tessa looked around. "You need a curio cabinet."

"It's on the list," Heather agreed. "There are several antique stores around here, and I was going to start shopping before all of this happened. I'll still shop but not as fast." Her ankle wouldn't be broken forever. It really was nice to have company. "There are four green glasses wrapped up in the bottom of that box." She'd found those on a trip to Portland.

Tessa instantly dug for them.

Donna looked around. "I say we do one room at a time instead of splitting up. Start with the kitchen?"

Three sets of very different colored eyes turned their focus on Heather. She knew when she was outnumbered, so she smiled. "Sounds good to me. Thank you." Since she'd put Quint in the friend zone, maybe she could be friends with his whole family, too.

For the first time in a month, she didn't feel so alone. "But I am buying lunch, and nobody gets to argue with me." It was probably a good idea to set limits with all of the Albertinis right off the bat.

Donna set her latte down and reached for a box on the floor. "We already ordered from Nordeliano's across town. We're distantly related."

Well. All right then.

* * *

LATE AFTERNOON, Heather looked around her newly put together office. It was perfect. The Albertini women had been great help, and Donna was an amazing organizer. By the end of the day, Heather felt like one of the family.

Anna sat on the floor, organizing file folders in the cabinet alphabetically. "You're dumb to put Quint in the friend zone." She didn't look up.

Heather started and then returned to organizing her pens in the top drawer. Donna and Tessa were finishing up in the guest room, so at least she didn't have to explain to all of them. "I'm not in a good place for a great guy like Quint." It was the easiest explanation.

Anna looked up, her eyes more green than gray in the soft sun coming through the wide window. "I get that. Is there a good place?" She frowned and looked back at the file folders. "I've found that when you find the guy, you create a good place. Well, probably. Heck. What do I know?"

Heather reached for a notepad to stack with the others near her computer. "Have you found the guy?"

"I think so," Anna said. "You'll meet Aiden, I'm sure."

It was so odd to feel such quick acceptance. It was nice, too. Heather was saved from answering when the door rang. "Please tell me you didn't order dinner as well?"

"Nope."

"I've got it," Donna called out from the living area. She returned moments later with a bouquet of red roses. "These are beautiful." Searching through them, she frowned. "No card."

Heather's abdomen cramped. Heat rushed to her temples. Jack had found her. Her address. Did he have a private detective or what? She couldn't put it past him. "I'm sure they just forgot the card," she said, her hands starting to shake.

Anna lifted an eyebrow. "Not Quint. He's not a rose type of guy. Right?"

"Right," Donna agreed, turning the roses around. "Plus, he'd leave a card." She focused on Heather. "Do you have a secret admirer?"

"No," Heather said, keeping her voice level. Jack was anything but a secret, although since she couldn't prove anything, he was good at being secretive.

Anna shut the file drawer and stood, stretching her back. "Did you see who delivered them?"

"Yeah. It was one of the Melanetti kids. He works for Jenny's Flowers." Donna angled her head. "I can call Jenny and ask who bought them. It's probably just a neighbor and she might've forgotten the card? Or the kid dropped it. Happens all the time."

"That'd be great," Heather said, turning in the office chair. Had Jack left a trail? She'd been keeping a notebook of all odd occurrences since they'd broken up, and if she could tie him to the roses, it'd be the first real proof she had that he wouldn't leave her alone. Or maybe the flowers were from some welcoming neighbor, and she was chasing ghosts again.

"Sure thing. I'll put them in water before I dig my phone out of my purse in the kitchen." Donna hustled out of the room.

Silence thickened.

"So. Who are you afraid of?" Anna asked, her gaze intelligent.

Heather rolled her eyes. "Nobody. I swear, you Albertini folks are an inquisitive bunch."

Anna chuckled. "You have no idea. I take it Quint already asked."

"Yes," Heather sighed. "I have an ex-boyfriend who is persistent, but I thought he'd give up when I moved so far north. In fact, I don't even think he really knows where I am. My imagination is overactive sometimes. I'm a writer/illustrator and it comes with the job." She hoped. Even so, that pit in her stomach wouldn't dissipate.

"What has the ex done?" Anna asked.

They couldn't keep calling him the ex. "His name is Jack, and when I broke things off, he started calling a lot. Texting about our future. Sometimes he was cajoling and sometimes he got angry. Never threatening—at least not obviously. Then he started showing up wherever I was, and it just got creepy, but I couldn't point to anything he did that would get him in trouble." Moving had been the best thing to do, especially since she wanted to live near her Grandma and was ready for a change anyway.

Anna grinned. "Let Quintino talk to him. Quint can be intense when he wants."

Heather laughed. "I can see that, but Quint is a nice guy who rescues stranded hikers in his free time. Other than that, he works in the forests managing trees, where it's peaceful and quiet. The last thing he needs is to deal with my problems."

Anna blinked. "Managing trees?"

"Yeah. He's a forestry technician, right?" Heather thought back to what Quint had told her. "I figured that means managing the forests and all of that."

"Oh." Anna twisted her lip, obviously thinking. "I think there's more to being a forestry technician than planting trees."

Heather leaned forward, hastening to reassure Anna. "I'm sure there is—honest. Quint seems amazing, and I'm sure he carries a lot of responsibility. I didn't mean to sound like he wasn't brave or wasn't doing anything worthwhile. He is. The forests are important to us all." In fact, Quint seemed like a fantastic man. He'd be a good friend, but she wasn't going to take advantage of his good nature.

Or kiss him. Everything about Quint Albertini screamed he'd be a phenomenal kisser.

She mentally slapped herself in the head. Why had her mind gone right there? She had to get control of her imagination as well as her libido, for goodness sakes. "What I'm saying is that your cousin has obviously carved himself out a nice and peaceful life here in northern Idaho, and I don't want to mess with that."

"What cousin?" Donna asked, moving back inside the office.

"Quint," Anna said on a half snort.

Donna stopped short. "Nice and peaceful life? Quint?"

"As a forestry technician, which is his job title, I think." Anna's smile made her eyes sparkle.

Heather looked between the sisters. "What am I missing?"

Donna laughed. "I think you'll have to ask Quint that." Then she sobered. "I just talked to Jenny, and the person paid with a prepaid visa over the internet form, and in the comment section said they wanted the flowers to be anonymous but you'd know who they were from."

Heather's lungs compressed. "I have an idea." So Jack had found her. What now?

CHAPTER 5

Quint took the dish from Heather and helped her into the truck, where Zena greeted her with a soft bark from the backseat. "Please tell me you're not angry." He had been interfering when he'd sent the cousins over to help, and from the sounds of it, Heather already had an unwelcome stalker in her life. "I thought you'd like to meet some folks from here, and those three are pretty great friends to have."

Heather pulled her seatbelt on after setting her tote bag to the side of her feet. Light snow covered her shoulders just from the walk to the truck. "It was nice of you and I enjoyed getting to know your cousins." Today she'd dressed in jeans with a pretty blue blouse and cardigan set, but there were slight circles beneath her eyes. Had she not slept? He returned her dish to her. "Thanks."

"Sure." He shut the door and walked slowly around the front of the truck, lecturing himself mentally the whole time. Most people didn't like interference like his family did, and he could only be friends with this woman. In other words, he needed to back the hell off, although it went against his nature. If she was scared, he'd take care of the threat. It was kind of what he did overall, but he didn't have a right in this situation. So he opened his door, slid inside the truck, and started the engine. Then he paused. "That smells delicious." The round dish was filling the cab of the truck with the smell of...what?

"Thanks." She held the dish securely. "I wasn't sure what to bring, so I made my Grandma's secret artichoke dip. The crackers are in the bag." She bit her lip. "If that's okay?"

"Of course," he said, smoothly driving down the quiet road. "I'm trying really hard to mind my own business here."

She sighed. "Your cousins told you about the roses?"

"Yep. I have no problem talking to this guy for you, if you want." He took the back roads toward the main river road, enjoying the beginning of the autumn colors outside.

"You think I can't handle it?" she murmured.

Warning. Back off. Flag on the play. "Heather? You're organized, smart, and obviously capable. So yeah, you can handle it, I'm sure." He slowed down as a couple of wild turkeys meandered along the side of the road, slugging through the thickening snow on the ground. "But sometimes a guy like this one, at least like he sounds, needs somebody his size to discuss matters with him. It's a fact, and I was just offering."

"That's kind of you, but I've got this." She watched another set of turkeys. Big ones. "Any heads up about what we're walking into with this barbecue?

Humor smashed into him and he chuckled. "Like I said, you're smart. All right. The family barbecue is at Donna, Tessa, and Anna's parent's house, so you'll get both sides of their family—the Irish and the Italian. Well, depending on who can make it. Since it's a nice day without too much snow falling, we'll be outside with heaters spread around the lawn, and there will be too much food, plenty of joking, and probably some lawn games. Oh. And matchmaking. A whole lot of it."

"I could fake a fiancé," she offered, her lips twitching.

God, she was cute. And she filled out that sweater set like it had been sewn for her. He loved full-bodied women. *Whoa. Left* turn. *Back to friend zone.* "That's a great thought, but you're too late. They know you're not engaged."

"We can handle this," she said to the white dish in her hands.

"Hope springs eternal," he said dryly, turning down the long drive to his aunt and uncle's house. There were already plenty of rigs lining the drive and a bunch of teenagers played snow volleyball toward the side of the sprawling log-style home. The river sparkled on the back side, winding around with some ice already forming near the banks. He parked up near the driveway, much closer than usual since Heather had to use the crutches he'd placed in the backseat.

Her phone buzzed from her bag and the atmosphere changed.

He looked at her now pale face. "Want me to answer it?"

She took it out and 'unknown number' showed on the screen. "Isn't that a bad idea? Every episode of *Stalker Snapped* I've seen on television proves that the bad guy is energized by what he or she considers competition."

Quint rubbed his smooth jawline. Since he'd shaved that morning, it wouldn't be smooth for long. "I have no idea." He'd never dealt with a stalker and would much rather just find this guy and punch him in the face. Twice. "Or maybe he'll give up?"

"I'm sure he'll give up," she said, sounding pretty certain. "He wasn't the most motivated of guys, and no doubt he's just bored right now. Although, the roses were a surprise. Up to this point, he has just called and texted, and the unknown number is new. I'm not sure what to do." She bit her lip. "I can't call the police since Jack hasn't really threatened me, and it isn't fair to get you involved."

"I am involved," Quint said quietly.

"Let's just go in." She rejected the call and shoved the phone back into the tote with the crackers and napkins.

"All right." Quint waved to the kids playing volleyball in the snow and then helped Heather out with her crutches, taking the dish and throwing the bag over his shoulder. "It was nice of you to bring food." Unnecessary, but very nice. The grandmas would love that.

She looked toward the wide front door and winced.

Yep. She was definitely smart. He chuckled. Why did she have to be so alluring? "Don't worry. Once the food is out, everyone concentrates on eating." He'd made sure to plan their arrival close to that time.

"Good." She flashed him a smile and hobbled along the shoveled path on the crutches to the door, which opened right before they got there.

"Hi, mom." Quint leaned down for a kiss, not surprised she'd been waiting for him. "This is Heather." His mom had light brown hair, deep brown eyes, and a smile that made almost everything okay.

She reached for Heather in a gentle hug. "We're glad you could make it. What smells so delicious?"

Quint handed over the round dish while Heather described it.

"How lovely." His mom ushered Heather inside, her eyes now way too sparkly. She leaned up to Quint, and her smile slid away. "Keep your cool. Both Jolene and Chrissy are here." With that bombshell, she turned and walked alongside Heather. "It's wonderful to meet you. You'll have to tell me all about your trek down the mountain with Quint. It sounds so romantic."

Quint watched them go, his mind spinning. Why the hell were Jolene and Chrissy at the barbecue? Oh, he'd only dated Jolene for a week, but he and Chrissy had been on and off again for a year until finally being completely done three months ago.

Everything inside him wanted to rush back to the car.

Zena looked up at him, waiting.

He sighed. "Let's do this, girl." Then he strode inside like he was diving into the deep end of the river head first.

* * *

HEATHER WOULD NEVER BE able to keep track of names or faces; there were so many. The back yard was wide and huge with too many picnic tables to count, leading down to the slowly grinding river. Even though there was a couple of inches of snow on the ground, there were big restaurant styled heaters set near each table that seemed to keep folks warm. Reindeer made up of sparkling lights and Santas were dotted all around. Trees and wild grasses sprang up along the far bank, giving the place a sense of tranquility. Except for all the people milling around.

Anna rescued her from questions peppered at her from a couple of uncles, two paper plates in her hands. "Let's get food and I'll take you to my table."

Heather stumbled up the stairs to the wooden deck, where a long table was ladened with platters of food on top of a red gingham tablecloth. "You all have your own tables?"

"No, but Pauley and I always sit at a little table closer to the river and off to the side. It has its own heater above us, and it's cozy, even though this is probably the last barbecue outside until spring. We need quiet." Anna started dishing up the plates. "Is there anything you don't like or should I just go for an assortment?"

"I like it all," Heather admitted, seeing her dish placed near the crackers. A large, very large man with blue eyes was scooping a healthy amount onto a plate.

Anna coughed. "Uncle Sean, save some for the rest of us."

Sean took another scoop. "I love artichoke dip, and you know it. Be faster if you want some."

Heather smiled to herself, even though she felt like a dork. Then she looked around. Where had Quint gone?

Anna finished piling the plates high with chicken, salads, more salads, and some interesting looking fruit dishes, along with Heather's appetizer.

Heather swallowed. "I'll never eat all of that."

Anna laughed. "You'll be surprised. It's all so good. Follow me."

They wound across a shoveled path and through people, stopping for Heather to meet several of them. Finally, they arrived at a round barrel of a table beneath a sweeping pine bough by the river. A tall heater glowed a bright orange above it. A teenager sat nearest the river with a plate in front of him. He had dark hair, soft brown eyes, and a clean-cut countenance.

"Pauley, this is Heather," Anna said, sitting in the middle

"Hi," Heather said, taking the final seat and putting her crutches on the ground next to her.

Pauley looked at her and then away. "Hello, Heather. Heather. Heather is a name and a plant in the genus Calluna." He rocked back and forth, looking at the river. "As well as current slang for somebody your crush likes. On TikTok." He looked at the neatly divided food on his plate.

"I knew about Calluna but not TikTok," Heather said, settling more comfortably on her seat as the heat warmed her from above. Pauley seemed Autistic, but she didn't know enough about it to know for sure.

"You are probably too old to know about TikTok," Pauley said, reaching for his fork.

Anna grinned and then dug into her food. "P thinks anybody over the age of twenty is old."

"Relatively," Pauley agreed.

Heather let the December sun and the nice heater warm her as she tasted her chicken and watched the mingling family members. "I like your table."

"It has three people," Pauley said. "Three. Three people. Three." He looked at Anna and then away. "Usually Anna and me and somebody else. Not Aiden today."

"Aiden?" Heather asked.

Anna pointed toward a group of men near an open metal container with ice and drinks. "Tall guy to the right."

Wowza. Aiden was at least six-four with dark hair and very wide shoulders. His face was rugged and strong. As if sensing their appraisal, he turned, and his eyes were a combination of too many blues to just be called blue. "Wow," Heather breathed.

Anna nodded. "Amen, sister."

"How long have you dated?" Heather asked. They made a nice couple.

"Not long and we keep spending a lot of time apart because if his job. We're new and finding our way, but we're getting there." Anna took another bite of a salad. "He just got back to town, and we're trying to find a rhythm. Although I think he might be a sociopath."

Heather choked on a crouton. "Really?"

Anna snorted. "Yeah. I'm helping him organize his new place, and he keeps combining three cereals into one container. Three different kinds. You'd have to be crazy to do that, right?"

"Absolutely," Pauley agreed. "Crazy."

Heather smiled. "I'm not sure. By the look of him, I'd say you might want to let that one flaw go."

Anna laughed.

Tessa bounded up with drinks. She wore a heavy blue jacket and mittens. "I have two wines and an orange juice for you, Pauley." She handed over the glasses to each of them. "I chose a white, if that's okay."

"Looks great," Heather said, taking her glass. "Thank you."

Tessa leaned in. "Did you see that both Jolene and Chrissy are here? Is Quint hiding or what?"

Heather took another sip and looked around. "I've heard about Jolene and understand their relationship was over quickly. Who's Chrissy?" Not that she cared. Nope. Not at all. Even so, she scouted the crowd for another hot blonde with big boobs.

Pauley sighed. "I am done. Gossip is boring." He grasped his plate, stood, and walked toward the deck and house that was decorated with too many Christmas lights to count.

Tessa immediately slid into his seat, her glass in hand. "Quint and Chrissy dated on and off for a year and broke up months ago.

She's nice and all but too demanding, and she couldn't handle his job. The travel of it."

Anna leaned closer and lowered her voice conspiratorially. "They weren't a good match, anyway. She's lovely, but they just didn't fit very well. I think they'd make great friends, though." Then she growled. "Why the hell is Jolene here? She keeps trying to bury me in the paper."

"Her cousin Melissa is dating one of the Coolie cousins, and somehow she tagged along. Just ignore her," Tessa said.

Heather didn't want to ask. Nope. She wouldn't. "Which one is Chrissy?" Yep. She'd asked. Weak.

Anna nodded toward a full-bodied blonde woman near the swing set. She was dressed in dark jeans with a light sweater, and her hair was up in a ponytail. "That's her. I guess she's dating Trick O'Leary? He's like a fifth cousin twice removed or something like that. He's over playing horseshoes."

"Kind of uncool to bring her," Tessa said, reaching across Heather to snag a roll from Anna's plate. Then she paused. "Mom's waving. I'll go help her." She darted off.

Heather ate more of her salad and tried not to watch the pretty blonde. It became more difficult when Chrissy turned, caught her eye, and then made her way toward them.

"Oh man," Anna murmured against her glass. "This is going to be interesting."

CHAPTER 6

$\mathcal{H}$eather smiled at the woman when she reached the table. "Hi."

"Heather, this is Chrissy," Anna said, taking another bite of fruit. "Chrissy, Heather. Would you like to sit with us?"

"Hi." Chrissy smiled and took Tessa's vacant seat. "I hope it's okay I'm here. I thought I shouldn't come, but Trick really wanted me to, and we've been dating for a month, so…" Her pink painted lips pursed.

Anna smiled across Heather. "You're welcome any time. I had no idea you and Trick have been dating for a month."

Chrissy visibly relaxed. "Yeah. We're taking it slow and all, but he's a really great guy."

Anna nodded. "I agree. Have you talked to Quint?"

Heather took another sip of her wine, wedged between the two women. Was this weird? Yeah, this was weird. Even so, she kept her smile in place.

Chrissy swallowed. "Not yet. I've been trying to get up the nerve, but I didn't want it to be awkward."

In that second, Heather liked the woman. She relaxed. "He's such a nice guy. I'm sure it'll be fine. Was the breakup…difficult?"

Why had she asked that? It wasn't her business. What was she doing?

Chrissy chuckled. "Not really. He is a nice guy, right? We knew we weren't meant for each other, and I just couldn't handle his crazy schedule and worrying about him all the time. But we got along and should've just stayed friends. I hope we can be."

"You can," Anna said, reaching over to pat Chrissy's hand. "It always seemed like you guys were friends, anyway."

Chrissy's smile came more naturally now. "Yeah." She nudged Heather. "But you two look good together. I heard all about the dramatic rescue down the mountainside. What a meet-cute, right?"

Heat flowed into Heather's face. "No. We're friends, that's all." She frowned. "Why were you so worried about Quint's job? I know he has to travel to other US Forests, but how dangerous can that be?"

Chrissy coughed hard on her wine.

The man in question loped up, bottles of water in his hands. He gave them over. "Nonna wants you all to drink water. You okay, Chris?"

Heather tried to remain calm. Did he still like his ex? Not that it mattered to her. But still, he was hot, and a hero, and he'd brought Heather to the picnic.

Anna jumped up. "Take my seat. I'll make sure everyone has water." She hurried off.

Heather watched her go, fighting the urge to hop after her. Traitor. "Um, thanks."

"Sure." He studied her heated face. "You okay?"

Of course. It wasn't every day she sat next to a hot guy's ex. A hot guy who she really wanted to see naked. That thought had to stop spinning through her head.

"Heather?" he prodded.

"I'm good," she said, reaching for the water. There wasn't enough in the bottle to cool her head, and if she poured it over her hair, everyone would probably think she was nuts. If she had to spend much more time around Quint and keep him in the friend zone, she would go crazy. But it was the right thing to do.

Chrissy sat straighter. "I hope it's okay I'm here, Quint. I should've called to talk to you first, but Trick really wanted to come, and I didn't think."

Quint turned to her, and his smile made his stunning eyes nearly glow. "Chris, come on. You know you are welcome any time, and I'm glad you're here. It's nice to see Trick with somebody as great as you."

Chrissy breathed out. "Okay. That's good. I'm so glad. I love these barbecues."

Quint claimed Anna's hastily vacated seat and stretched his legs out, crossing his boots at the ankles. "Me, too."

Heather looked from one to the other, sitting between them. "Do you guys want to talk? I can go help Anna."

"Nope," Chrissy said. "We're all good. Just relax." She looked at Quint. "I heard you were injured last month. All healed?"

Quint nodded. "Yeah. No worries. I'm good."

"Injured?" Heather asked. The guy had carried her down a mountain, and it wasn't like she was a lightweight. "What injury?"

Quint shrugged. "Just a little one from a recent job. No big deal."

"No big deal?" Chrissy burst out. "You are crazy. You know that?" Her smile was good-natured and rather relieved. "I heard your parachute got caught and spun you in the wrong direction."

"True." Quint leaned down and snapped his fingers as Zena ran toward them. The dog instantly lay down at his feet, partially beneath the table.

Heather reached for the wine instead of water. "Parachute? You're a forestry technician."

Chrissy took a drink of her water. "I always thought that was too casual of a job description for a smokejumper."

Now Heather coughed out wine. "You're a smokejumper? I

mean, you parachute into the middle of forest fires?" Her voice rose and she quickly lowered it.

Quint nodded. "Sure."

Chrissy leaned toward her. "He won't brag, but he's also a rappeller, although he prefers the smoke jumping." She shook her head. "Talk about an adrenaline junkie."

"I am not," Quint said, resting his hand on Zena's head. "I just get the job done."

Chrissy waved at Trick, who gestured her toward the horseshoe area. "Oh. I'm up. Wish me luck." She took her water with her.

Quint settled back. "How weird was that for you?"

Heather burst out laughing.

* * *

QUINT SMILED. The woman had a great laugh. "You're a good sport, Heather Davis." Yet one more thing to appreciate about the pretty blonde.

"Thanks. Are all of your exes so good-natured with you?" Heather asked, her small hands playing with her wineglass.

He patted the dog's head and mused. "I think so, actually. I've even served as a groomsman in a couple of ex-girlfriend's weddings." At her second laugh, he smiled again. "Is that odd?"

"Yeah, but sweet." She sipped her wine.

The sight of her full bottom lip on the wineglass zipped right to his groin, and he shifted his weight. "That's me. Sweet." He'd been called a lot of things in his life, and sweet was not one of them. Even by his mama. "Absent, irritable, dangerous, and selfish are the adjectives tossed at me during arguments while dating. Then we become friends afterward...usually right around the time an ex starts dating either a friend or a relative." He glanced over at Trick and Chrissy.

Heather patted his thigh, probably not knowing that she'd just

43

killed him because his cock nearly exploded. "I can't see you being selfish."

"When the job calls, it calls." He scratched behind Zena's ears and the dog grunted in pleasure. It felt right being here with Heather, and he knew better. In fact, since it was early December, he more than likely would be leaving town any day again since there were still fires in California right now. "I don't control forest fires, but when one springs up, I go. I've found that girlfriends don't like that schedule very much." Oh, someday he'd stick closer to home, especially if he had kids, but now wasn't that time. Now was the time to beat fire and win. Or at least tie.

"I see." Heather rested her chin on her hand and watched a boisterous game of darts played on a snowy tree away from the tables. "I can understand a little bit. When I get into a book, really drawing the pictures, I go into my own head for a while. I've been told I need to be more present, but I guess so far, I'd rather be in my book."

If her current ex was anything to go by, Quint didn't blame her. "I haven't read your books yet."

"They're for toddlers and grade school kids," she said, a dimple appearing in her left cheek. "I'd be worried if you had read them." Her gaze sharpened as Jolene walked on too high heels toward them. Her boots kept sinking into the snow.

Jolene reached them, her professional smile in place. "It is so nice to see you again, Heather. I was hoping you'd reconsidered the story. It's a good one."

Heather swallowed. "That's kind of you, but I'd prefer to stay under the radar as a new person in town. I'm sure there are hikers who are saved all the time by Search and Rescue."

Quint understood. Apparently her ex had found her, and she no doubt wanted to keep her life private.

"Yes, but they're not normally invited to the Albertini family barbecue," Jolene said, her tongue moistening her lips. "If this is a romance, that'd make a fantastic human interest story." Her gaze slashed to Quint, blatant interest glowing in her eyes.

Heather stiffened. "I don't have a comment."

Jolene put a manicured hand on her hip. "Quint? What about you? What about a feature about Zena and you?"

"No." Quint didn't elaborate.

Heather shifted in her chair. Was her ankle bothering her again? Quint could find her an aspirin around there somewhere.

Jolene raked his body with her gaze, and he didn't feel a thing. "Well, just think about it. You have my number, Quint." She turned and walked across the lawn, somehow making her ass sway even as her heels stuck in the frost covered grass.

Heather tried to bite her lip. "We both have her number."

Humor rippled through Quint.

"I don't like when women fight each other or make each other feel badly," Heather said. "I believe in the sisterhood and in building each other up. We're not competing with each other, and I really dislike cattiness."

"And?" Quint asked dryly.

Heather exhaled. "That woman sets me on edge. I wish she didn't want to write a story about me."

He nodded. "Same here."

She managed to keep the question in for a couple of seconds, but he knew it was coming. He could feel it.

"You mentioned that you were in a bad place when you hooked up with Jolene. Was it because you were injured?" She finally asked.

His gut ached. "No. Part of Zena's training is to search for survivors as well as the deceased after a fire. In that fire, we didn't find any survivors."

"Oh." Her voice softened. "I'm sorry."

"Me, too." It had been ugly, and he wasn't going to talk about it. "That's the other thing that makes me bad at relationships right

45

now." Considering he wanted to kiss her the sweeter she got, it was only fair to warn her.

She turned to face him fully. Those eyes were unreal. Green didn't come close to describing them. "What?"

"I don't bring it home." There wasn't much more of an explanation than that. "Sometimes I get home and need a few days to decompress, and the last thing I want to talk about is dead and burned bodies. Ever." He had to keep this place, *his home*, clear of that pain. Period.

"I can understand that." She looked past him to the dog. "I hadn't realized dogs could find bodies after a fire."

He leaned to the side to make sure Zena still had water in her bowl by the deck. "Not only can this princess find bodies after a fire, she can also find cremated ashes *in* fire ashes. Like if somebody had an urn on their mantle and their house burned down, she could find the actual ashes from the urn."

"Really?" Heather's brow furrowed, and she searched his eyes for the joke.

"Yeah," he said softly. "It's pretty amazing, really. They actually smell the ground-up bone matter from the cremated remains." That reminded him that he needed to buy more dog treats on the way home. Zena had definitely earned them. "They're good at finding historical remains, too. That's not our focus, though."

Heather looked at him like he was something intriguing. He could get used to that look. "Your focus is parachuting into a forest fire," she murmured.

"Yeah." He grinned. "Or I rappel down if necessary, but I'd much rather jump."

Her answering smile slammed through his chest stronger than an anvil. Oh, he was in trouble with this one. He forced himself to look away, only to see his Nonna smiling at them from across the lawn.

His sigh was silent.

CHAPTER 7

$\mathcal{I}$t was dark by the time Quint drove her home, and Heather had to fight to keep her eyelids open. After not sleeping well the night before, the day had been fun and tiring. So she didn't argue when he lifted her out of the truck and carried her to the front door through a walkway that needed to be shoveled. She'd have to find a local kid to hire. "What is it with you carrying me?" she asked, trying not to snuggle right into his broad chest.

"I find it easier to get from point A to point B when I'm in charge," he said, using her key to open the door. His breath was minty and his arms strong. He also didn't sound like he was joking.

She chuckled anyway. "I like the way your mind works."

He stepped inside and flicked on the light. "That's what you think."

Awareness flickered to life along her nerve endings. "What do you mean?" She tilted her head back to see his face, and her gaze immediately dropped to his firm looking lips. He had great lips.

His sigh showed he was on the same wavelength. "Heather."

"Yeah." She tangled her hand in his thick hair, noting that even

47

his neck felt strong. Her body was tired and her mind fuzzy, but she knew what she wanted. So she leaned up and kissed him.

Just one taste. She only wanted one taste.

He stiffened, even as she traced the contours of his mouth.

Then he kissed her back.

Wildfire heated her veins, igniting her cells, throwing her into an inferno. She curled her fingers tighter into his silky hair and moaned into his mouth.

His hold tightened around her, his arm beneath her knees and the one banded around her shoulders, keeping her exactly, gently, firmly where he wanted her.

He tasted like whiskey and minty coffee, and her mouth automatically opened beneath his, letting him deepen the kiss.

Gone was the good ole boy who'd joked with her, and in its place was a dangerous force of pure masculinity. Oh, she'd sensed the depths of Quintino Albertini, but she hadn't considered she'd be plundered by them.

Intensity and control surrounded her, took her. She shivered against him, wanting more but needing to hide the desperate, hungry part of her that didn't belong in a friendship.

His tongue scraped hers, and he completely took over, submerging her into so much pleasure that she just relaxed and let him take. Whatever he wanted. Heat flowed through her, and she softened against him, her blood pounding so hard through her veins that it hurt. Her body ached. Everywhere for him—for his touch.

He lifted his mouth, and his eyes had darkened to a mysterious brown flecked with tawny spikes. His nostrils flared and the desire stamped hard on his face.

She swallowed, unable to move. The muscles holding her had gone rigid, and his expression hot.

In that second, she felt vulnerable, feminine, and somehow powerful. Oh, she could dive right into the sensations and worry about consequences later.

Her phone buzzed from her bag.

She jolted.

His frown held thunder clouds. "It's a little late on a Sunday for a call. Want me to handle it?"

Handle it. Something told her Quint could pretty much handle anything, including *her* right now. She took a deep breath. "You're like a chocolate chip infused donut with glazed icing," she whispered, her nipples peaking and her clit pounding from just one kiss.

One of his dark eyebrows rose. "Excuse me?"

She ignored the buzzing phone and slowly untangled her fingers from his hair. "Delicious and tempting, but I'd regret it in the morning when I tried to put my jeans back on."

His chuckle was soft but did nothing to take away from the predatory gaze in his eyes. "Honey, if I got you into bed, you'd still be naked all the next morning. Trust me."

A tremble took her, head to toe, and hit all the spots in between.

His flash of a grin showed he'd felt every stop on the way. "I'd like to stay."

"You know that's a mistake." Oh, she wanted him to stay. They didn't even have to make it to the bedroom. The old sofa looked plenty comfortable. Never in her entire life had she been kissed like that. Never.

"I'm not so sure," he said, a new light in his eyes. "Might not be a mistake." Even so, he gently set her on one foot.

She grasped his forearms until she regained her balance. Kind of. "Um, friend zone? Remember?" Her body didn't care. At all.

"Hmm." He looked at her again, his gaze probing. "Like I said, I'm not sure about that." He turned on his heel to go back to his truck and dog, stopping on the other side of the door and grasping the shovel leaning against the side. "Lock this and call me if you have any problems." He'd made sure they'd exchanged numbers at the barbecue, and he was already safely in her contacts. "Promise me."

"Sure." She hopped over to him. The biggest problem in her life at the moment was her insane desire to beg him to stay the night. Although, what could it hurt?

Except her heart. Oh yeah. That. He'd been more than clear that he wasn't ready for a relationship, and she'd never been able to do the casual thing. Quint would probably be worth the heartache, though.

He reached over and tucked her hair behind her ear.

She caught her breath and tried to look calm. "Thank you for taking me to the barbecue. I really like your family." Yet another reason not to end up in an awkward morning after situation with him. She wanted to spend more time with the Albertini family members.

"Thanks for going." He looked at her lips again and then slowly shut the door between them. "Lock it," he said clearly.

"You're bossy," she muttered, engaging the deadbolt.

He chuckled and the low tone rumbled through the door. "You have no idea." Then he quickly shoveled her walkway before his footsteps faded away.

Oh, she had some idea after that kiss, and now she wanted more.

Her phone buzzed again from her purse. She hopped to it, yanked it free, and pressed the screen to her ear. "What?"

"It's about time you answered," Jack said, his voice irritable. "Where have you been?"

She hobbled over to the sofa and dropped onto it. It was time he got the message. "Listen, Jack. We are not dating, we are not friends, and I don't want to talk to you ever again. I really don't understand why you won't get the message." Hadn't she been clear enough?

His sigh was like fingernails across a blackboard. One of the old green kinds. "I know you're upset about your grandmother and not thinking clearly, so I'm not going to get my feelings hurt."

"I couldn't give two fucks about your feelings," she burst out. "Honestly. Listen to me. I do not care how you feel. All I want is for you to leave me alone." Enough was enough. She extended her legs to the antique coffee table.

"You know I don't like it when you swear," he said lowly.

She snorted. "Fuck you, Jack. We're done. Don't send flowers and don't call any longer." She'd add that he shouldn't key her car again, but that'd just start an argument where he'd deny it and accuse her of being paranoid, and she'd say he was a liar, and that would just keep them on the phone. "Goodbye."

"Wait. We dated for six months. How can you just throw that away?" Now he sounded whiny.

She shook her head. What had she been thinking? He'd seemed charming and smart until he'd gotten too, well, persistent. "It's done. I'm not answering the phone again."

"Is it because of the guy with the dog?"

She stilled. Her body chilled. "Excuse me?"

"The big dumb hick with the dog in the truck. Do you really think you can move on from me to him?" The whine disappeared.

She eyed the deadbolt and ran through the list of knives in the kitchen. She didn't have a gun. Yet. "Are you spying on me?" Hopefully he'd just hired somebody.

"Of course not. Why are you so paranoid?" Now he sounded calm again.

She bit her tongue until she could keep her voice placid. Her lungs fought her but she kept breathing smoothly. "I'm not playing games, Jack. Are you watching me?" What was he doing in northern Idaho? How long had he been there? Was Quint in danger? Was she?

"I am not spying on you. But you don't think you're going to start dating a mountain man, do you? Get serious, Heather. You and I belong together. You know that. Don't make me show you."

Bile rolled around in her belly. "If you keep bothering me, I will call the police." She ended the call and set the phone next to her on the sofa.

Then she waited.

After about fifteen minutes, she stood and double-checked that the doors and windows were all locked, hopping around the house. Then she chose several knives from the kitchen and went to her bedroom, locking that door and stashing the knives where she could get to them easily.

Then she shook her head. Maybe she was a little paranoid.

Even so, she got settled onto her knees to push a dresser in front of the door, knowing she wouldn't get a second of sleep until she got it into place. Her cast rested on the wooden floor, and she was careful not to twist her injured ankle while pushing with her arms and torso. Then she grasped the side of the dresser and pulled herself up.

What about the window?

It faced the fenced back yard, trees, and quiet creek. A bar attached to the base kept it from being forced open. If Jack somehow tried to break the glass, she'd awaken for sure. Although she needed to get her hands on a gun.

Was she overreacting?

Probably.

But she'd rather be safe than sorry. She looked at the phone she'd placed on her bedside table. The urge to call Quint was overwhelming, and not just because he'd probably kiss her again. Although if Jack had gone nutty, she was placing Quint in danger by just hanging out with him.

She needed to stop watching *Stalker Snapped* on the crime channel. Her imagination was going too wild. Jack was an ass who had a big ego she'd dented, and he was just messing with her. Although, either he was having her watched, or he actually was in town, so his actions had elevated him to a threat. Maybe a dorky one, but sometimes people went crazy.

Was she being stalked, or was she overreacting? Either way, Jack hadn't done anything yet that she could put in a police report. Unless following her to Silverville counted, and she doubted that was enough. Even so, she'd go down to the station in the morning and file a preliminary report or whatever they were called. Just in case.

Yeah. She really did have to stop watching true crime shows.

After she got a gun.

CHAPTER 8

*Q*uint reached his cabin and sighed at seeing the woman sitting on the front porch swing his mama had insisted he install. The eaves protected her from the falling snow. Zena looked up from the passenger seat, and her tail didn't wag. "I know. I should've listened to you," he murmured, opening his door and letting the dog jump to the ground. His body was on fire from kissing Heather, and his temper wasn't far behind.

Even so, he calmly shut his door and strode up his snowy walk. His Christmas lights were on and sparkling since he'd scheduled them on a timer. "Jolene? Why are you on my front porch?"

She'd wrapped herself in a heavy jacket, but her nose was red from the chilly evening. "I wanted to talk to you. You're home later than I expected." There was a clear question in the statement.

He shoved his hands in his pockets. "We don't have anything to talk about on a Sunday night. I really don't want to be featured in the newspaper." Chasing glory wasn't something he'd ever tried, even when he'd been a pretty good running back in high school and college. It was the strategy and joy of the game he'd loved. Now he loved fighting nature and outmaneuvering fires to help people. "You have to understand me that much."

"I understand you well enough." She stood and pushed away from the swing. "Are you going to ask me inside or not?"

"No, but I will walk you to your car." He glanced to see it parked on the side of his metal shop near the trees and out of the way. "Let's go."

She pouted her bright red lips and strode down the three wooden steps to stand in front of him. "I have a better idea. How about bourbon by the fireplace…inside?"

He fully planned to have a bourbon by the fire after she was on her way. "Come on." He turned with his hands still in his pockets to walk to her car, keeping his stride short so she could keep up in the heels.

She tottered next to him and slid her hand between his arm and his ribcage to hold on. "You're mean."

He sighed and kept walking. "No, I'm not. You wrote a hit piece on my cousin based on something I told you confidentially, and that ended things for us." Not that they'd been going anywhere, anyway. While he liked ambitious people, Jolene didn't care who she hurt, and he couldn't get on board with that.

"We're still friends, aren't we?" She pressed closer to him, and her breast brushed his upper arm.

"Not really." He'd learned a long time ago not to play games with women. Except chess. Did Heather play chess? He enjoyed the strategy of the game. She'd probably be pretty good at it.

Jolene huffed out air. "Fine. I'm sorry I wrote that story about Anna, but it was all true."

"True and slanted in a way to hurt her. What's your problem with Anna?" Quint reached the car and opened the driver's side door for her, wiping snow off the window with his hand.

"She makes for a good story," Jolene admitted, not looking at him.

Quint didn't care if Jolene still had the hots for Aiden because that guy was so wrapped up in Anna he couldn't see straight. In fact, Quint could feel a little sorry for him because Anna's life was anything but calm. Ever. "You might want to leave her alone," he suggested. "You and Aiden dated for a short time way back in high school, and you should leave the past where it belongs."

Jolene scoffed. "Please. I'm not writing stories about Anna because of Aiden. It's because of Anna."

Yeah, Quint could see that, too. "All right. Drive carefully home. This snow is only going to get thicker and the roads are already icy."

She released him and turned fully into him, her hands sliding up his chest. "I have a much better idea."

The wrong woman had her hands on him. He knew it without a doubt, and he was going to have to figure that out by himself at the fire.

Zena barked from the porch. Yeah, he definitely should've taken his cue from his dog. She'd never liked Jolene.

Quint gently extracted himself.

Zena barked louder.

That was odd. A truck rumbled up the drive, and Quint's instincts kicked in. He grabbed Jolene around the waist and threw them both over the hood of her car as bullets exploded against the metal. They landed on the snow-covered gravel, and pain burst through his elbow. She screamed and struggled beneath him.

He scrambled up and shoved her around the side. "Keep your back to the tire and your head down," he barked.

She whimpered and hunkered down.

He measured the distance to the house, where he could get a gun. Then he levered up to see the taillights of the truck speeding down his driveway and away. He could probably catch the guy. "Are you okay?" He stood, ready to run.

"No," she said, crying. "I think I was shot."

Shit. He forgot all about pursuit and rushed around the car, dropping to his haunches. "Where?" He gingerly ran his hand down her arms. She sat with her knees bent and her arms wrapped around them. "Are you bleeding?" Damn it. He needed to get her into the house where he could see. "Hold on." He lifted her and ran across the lawn toward the porch, clearing it and opening his door to rush inside, where he laid her on the sofa.

Then he flipped on the lights and returned to her. "Where are you hit?"

Her hair was all over and her eyes wide. She looked down at her jeans, which were ripped at the knees. Blood welled from them. "Oh. I'm sorry. I'm just scratched from the gravel." Was she going into shock?

He looked her over and then grabbed a blanket to cover her. "What hurts, Jolene? Were you hit?"

She slowly shook her head and cuddled into the blanket. "No. I don't think so."

He exhaled as relief buzzed through his veins. "Okay." Tugging out his phone from his back pocket, he quickly dialed 9-1-1.

It was too late to chase the shooter.

* * *

THE MORNING HALTED the freezing snowstorm for a least a little while. Heather used her crutches to make her way out of the brick building housing the Silverville City Police Department to find Anna Albertini leaning against her red Touareg, her nose red from the cold. "Anna? What's up?" She moved closer.

Anna straightened, today wearing jeans and a heavy green parka. "I saw your car. What's going on?" Her eyes were more gray than green today, and her brunette hair was up in a casual ponytail. "Is everything okay?"

"Yeah." Heather paused and stood on her good foot, straightening so the crutches didn't bite into her armpits.

Anna looked closer. "All right. How about breakfast? Sunshine Eats is just down the street."

On cue, Heather's stomach growled. "Sounds good. What are

you doing in Silverville? I thought you were headed over the pass last night for work."

Anna rolled her eyes and fell into step beside her. "I got called in and questioned because of the shooting at Quint's house last night. Can you believe that?"

Heather stumbled, and the ground fell out beneath her. "What? Quint was shot?" Panic grabbed her around the throat.

Anna stopped. "No. He's fine." She moved for the door to Sunshine's and opened it. "The sheriff is pretty sure the shooter was after Jolene, and Quint just happened to be there. Jolene has a few investigative stories in the hopper, and she thought she recognized the truck after she'd calmed down. Something to do with bank fraud." She gestured Heather inside the quiet family restaurant that had winter designs on all of the windows.

Heather's head spun and she hitched inside, moving for the nearest green booth to slide along the smooth leather. Christmas music tinkled in the background. Once Anna had seated herself, Heather stared at her. "Are you telling me that Jolene was at Quint's house. *Last night?*" After he'd kissed her?

Anna blinked and a slow smile tipped her lips. "Well, yeah. Apparently he got home and she was waiting for him. Then somebody shot at them from a truck that no longer had a license plate. You can't believe Quint is interested in Jolene any longer."

Couldn't she? Heather reached for a menu. It didn't matter to her. Even if Quint wasn't interested in Jolene, Heather had been smart to put him in the friend zone. Life was crazy right now, and it appeared that Quint's life included women who waited all night for him to show up. "What's good here?"

"Everything," Anna said.

Figured. They ordered from a cute waitress with purple hair before sipping happily on flavored coffee.

The door opened behind Heather with a tinkle of the bell above it, but she didn't turn around. Until the sheriff strode up to the table. "Miss Davis?"

She set her cup down and looked up at the grizzly older man. "Hi, Sheriff. Was there a problem with my report?" She'd placed a report about Jack and the flowers and phone calls with a younger deputy before meeting Anna on the street.

"No. We've had a report against you." He pushed back his cowboy hat to reveal thick white hair. "Sorry about that, but I need to take you in." He had a gun and badge at his belt, and even though he had to be in his late sixties, the man looked like he could take on a grizzly bear.

She blinked, and her stomach dropped. "A report against me? For what?"

"Vandalism and malicious mischief," the sheriff said. "You're on video destroying a couple of cars at Molly's Motel last night."

Anna burst out laughing. "She's on crutches, Sheriff."

He nodded, his faded eyes sober. "I know. She's on crutches in the video."

Anna lost the smile. "Heather?"

Heather's mouth gaped open, and she could only shake her head.

Anna's eyes sharpened. "All right. Let's see this video." She stood and handed Heather the crutches. "There's no way my client committed any of those crimes last night, Sheriff." She waited until Heather had bundled back into her coat before drawing on her own parka. "This is ridiculous."

Heather used the crutches to head out of the restaurant and down the salted and shoveled sidewalk to go back into the sheriff's building, her mind reeling. "Whose cars did I supposedly destroy?" Then her gaze caught sight of Jack sitting in the same chair she'd sat in earlier at the deputy's desk. "Oh, you have got to be kidding me," she muttered, the hair on the back of her neck rising. "Have you lost your mind?" she snapped.

Jack's light brown hair was wet from melting snow, and his eyes gleamed. "You can't do things like that, Heather. I know you're grieving from your grandmother's death, and I know you're not in your right mind, but you have to let me help you." He stood, earnestness spreading across a face she'd once considered handsome. He was tall and thin, and for the weather today he wore a brown coat, tan pants, and dark boots.

Anna cocked her head to the side. "Who are you?"

"Oh, sorry." He hurried forward and held out a hand. "I'm Jack Allen, Heather's boyfriend."

Anna shook his hand, her gaze appraising.

"Ex-boyfriend," Heather corrected, her armpits aching from the stupid crutches. "I have no idea what you're up to, Jack, but you need to stop it right now."

His face dropped in a sympathetic expression that made her want to vomit. "You're not in your right mind, honey."

Anna released his hand. "You do realize that filing a false police report carries jail time in Idaho?" Without waiting for an answer, she turned to the sheriff. "We'd like to see the video." She turned and strode through the hub of three desks to a conference room as if she knew exactly what she was doing.

Heather followed her, acutely aware of the sheriff behind her. When she sat in a dark leather chair by a well-worn table, she sighed and fought the urge to throw the crutches across the room. Stupid things.

The sheriff punched keys on a laptop, and the screen at the far end of the room lit up. Heather ducked her head to see better. A woman dressed in a dark coat like hers, with a hoodie covering her face and head, keyed a couple of cars in front of a hotel while the snow billowed down. She used crutches and took her time, and not once did her face show.

"That's Jack's SUV." Heather pointed to a blue SUV. "I don't know who owns the other car."

"A guy named Phil Lightenship who's in town from Helena," the sheriff said. "Is that you?"

Heather shook her head. "No. I don't move that well with the crutches." The woman was good at keeping her face off-camera.

"Although she's my size and that looks like my coat. Or at least it's close to my coat."

Anna sat back. "You don't have enough to arrest her, Sheriff. You can't tell who that is." She looked sideways at him. "I need a copy of that."

"I'll email it to you," he agreed, no expression on his gnarled face. "The complainant wants to talk to you. This would be so much easier if you all agreed that it wasn't you. What do you say?"

Heather shook her head, but Anna stopped her with a hand on her shoulder.

"Oh, bring him in," Anna said, her smile shark-like. "We'd love to talk to him."

Heather shivered.

CHAPTER 9

Snow fell lightly to continue covering the forest service road in the middle of nowhere. Silence abounded with peace and the sense of winter as the tree boughs filled with white around them. "I want to work on ballistics," Quint said, putting the collar on Zena next to his truck. "She can find shell casings and the wad, but I haven't had time to work with her lately to hunt down shells."

His brother finished securing the collar around his puppy. "Sounds good to me. Opal here is almost ready to start with search and rescue, but she needs a little tempering first." He patted the yellow lab on the head, and the dog yipped happily. "Or maybe a lot of tempering." Vince grinned. "I came out earlier and shot at a tree, so there's a shell casing to the north and the wad should be close to that nearest tamarack. Go for it."

Quint looked down at his dog. "Sit."

Zena sat, and her body vibrated. She wore the collar and not the search and rescue vest, so she should know what her job was today.

"Are you ready to work?" Quint asked.

She stiffened.

"Go to it. Find." He gestured toward the trees.

The dog took off, running in a zig-zag pattern. While her main focus would always be search and rescue or finding cadavers, sometimes Quint got the chance to assist the sheriff or local fish and game with cases, and Zena was one of the best at scouting.

Vince watched the dog go as his dog played around his boots. "Are you thinking of making a job change?"

A pit dropped into Quint's gut. "No. Well, I don't think so."

Vince's dark eyebrows rose nearly to his black hair. His eyes were a deep blue, unlike the rest of the brothers. "That was uncertain. What's up with you?"

Quint shrugged. "Find it, girl," he called out as Zena plunged into the trees.

Vince sighed. "Quint? Give."

Quint shoved his hands in his pockets against the freezing snow. "Someday I'm going to have to find another line of work. Not yet, but I don't know."

Vince rolled his eyes. "It's the new girl, isn't it?"

"She's a woman and not a girl," Quint said, easily deflecting.

"Whatever. You like her, but if she likes you, she won't get in the way of your job. You know that," Vince said, angling his head to better see Zena. "She's caught the scent."

Quint nodded. "Yeah. When Zena's tail wags like that, she's on to something. I've never met a woman who's okay with me leaving at any time and jumping into a fire."

"Maybe you have now," Vince said, turning the collar of his flannel coat up to cover his neck.

"It's too early to even think like that," Quint admitted. "I just met the woman."

Vince snorted. "Yet we know exactly who we're talking about." He clapped Quint on the shoulder. "You could always come work for us. We'd even make you a partner." Vince and a couple other brothers owned and ran an outfitting company for fishing, rafting, hunting, and guiding.

Quint grinned. "Maybe someday when I'm old and decrepit like you, I will want to run guides on the river."

"I'm three years older than you, jackass," Vince returned.

Zena barked once.

Quint immediately strode through the heavy snow and between trees until finding his dog lying down by the tree. "Where is it?" he asked.

She dug furiously in the snow and flipped over a shotgun shell.

"Good girl," he said, letting his voice rise so she knew he was happy. "Now find the wad. Go get it, girl."

She jumped up and started searching for the wad, which was released when a shotgun shell was fired. Then she flopped down.

He kicked through snow to reach her, seeing the wad stuck in the snow. "Good girl." He grabbed the throw toy off his belt and threw it for her.

She barked happily and ran for it, snatching the red triangle from the snow and bounding back toward him. They played fetch for about thirty minutes, and then he took her back to the truck to get warm and eat some grub.

Vince took the leash off his puppy. "Since Zena is taking a break, go get lost in the woods, would you? I want to see if she can find you."

"Sure." Quint's phone buzzed and he lifted it to his ear. "Albertini."

"Hey, it's Anna. We have a problem," his cousin said. "Any chance you can provide an alibi for Heather last night around midnight?"

Quint frowned. "I believe I was getting shot at during that time frame. Why does she need an alibi?"

He listened to the story and then slowly clenched his hand into a fist. "I think I should go have a talk with this asshole. He's staying at the Molly?"

"Don't even think it," Anna snapped. "I have it under control for now, but I do need you to get charming with the clerk at the motel. It's Diane Lewiston, and she's still mad at your brother for breaking up with her in high school, but I need you to go interview her and see if you can get any clue about who the vandal really was that night. Okay?"

He'd much rather go punch this Jack guy in the face. "I'll see what I can do." He clicked off to see his brother watching him carefully. "What?"

"You're way too invested in too short of a time, brother," Vince said calmly.

That was the damn truth. "I have to go."

Vince nodded. "It's not like the Albertinis are known for taking it slow, I guess. Never thought you'd dive head first into anything except a fire."

"I'm not diving into anything," Quint said, opening his door and tossing the toy inside. "I'm just helping out a friend."

Vince's laughter was familiar...and unrelenting.

* * *

HEATHER TRIED to school her expression into one of boredom, but her ears were tingling with heat, and her lungs kept compressing.

Anna returned to the conference room after having made a phone call outside and took a seat next to her. "Don't worry. We'll figure this out. I have a copy of the video and a couple of my friends are out and about trying to see what really happened that night. Let's deal with this today."

Jack sauntered into the room, his gaze instantly seeking Heather. "I hope we can reach a resolution here." He pulled out a chair on the opposite side of the table and looked at Anna. "If you don't mind, we'd like privacy."

"I do mind," Anna said, sounding official even though she was in jeans and a sweater. "I'm Heather's attorney, and I'm staying right here."

The sheriff gave them all a look that was a clear warning. "If there's trouble, I have no problem tossing all of you in a cell. Don't give me trouble." He shut the door as he left.

"I like him," Heather mused.

Anna nodded. "Yeah, he's pretty great." Her gaze didn't leave Jack's face. "In fact, he really doesn't like people messing with townspeople, and especially women. Oh, he's a softie, and it's probably old-fashioned, but he's very protective. You don't want to cross him, Jack."

Jack slowly turned his attention from Heather to Anna. "I'm not afraid of the sheriff."

"Then you're a dumbass," Anna said easily. "Even so, you should be afraid of me. I have no problem suing you for harassment on Heather's behalf, and I have connections to find any phone records you've left. Even those from a burner."

Heather wasn't certain that was possible, but Anna sure sounded confident. Maybe she was correct, or perhaps she was a great bluffer. Either way, it was nice to have her as a friend. "Did you really set all of this up, Jack?" she asked.

He sighed. "Are you having a breakdown? If so, I can get you help."

She shook her head. How could he look so concerned and genuine? Either a random woman on crutches damaged his car, or he set the whole thing up. Logically, he had to have set the entire situation up. "Listen. It's pretty much ridiculous to think that another woman on crutches wanted to harm you. Since I didn't do anything to your car, the only possible conclusion is that you hired some lady to do that. Why in the world would you do such a thing?" she asked, her ankle aching.

"You know I didn't do anything like that," he said, his voice almost gentle. "I think we just need a little time away. If you would just agree to spend a weekend with me in my cabin in Bozeman, then I'd drop these charges. It's a small thing to ask."

Before Heather could answer, Anna held up a hand. "Wait a minute," Anna said. "Just so I have this right. All Heather has to do is spend a weekend in Bozeman with you, and you'll drop everything?"

"Yes," Jack said.

Heather rounded on Anna. "You can't think this is a good idea."

"Nope," Anna said, reaching for a legal tablet on the table. "I'm just documenting that Jack here just committed extortion. Perfectly, actually." She lifted her gaze to a camera in the far corner. "On digital, no less." She settled back and crossed her legs, looking pretty damn happy. "Sometimes it's nice when things work out without my falling out of trees, you know?"

Jack looked at Anna like she was nuts, although he had gone a little pale. "I don't like being threatened."

"Who does, really?" Anna asked with a slight shrug. "Back to business. Who is the woman in the video, Jack?"

He crossed his arms. "I think it's obvious that Heather is in the video."

"Nope," Anna said. "Let's go back a bit. Why are you in Silverville staying at the Molly Motel?"

Jack lowered his chin and looked like a charging bull. "I came to Silverville to visit Heather after I learned that her grandmother died, and last night when we talked on the phone, she seemed sad and lost. I don't understand it, but Heather took that frustration out on my vehicle. It's heartbreaking, really."

Heather reared up. "So you admit we talked on the phone last night, Mr. Unknown Caller?" Yes! He'd admitted it on camera, too. Her nose itched, but since she now knew she was on camera, she so was not going to scratch it. It itched right inside, too. She cleared her throat and tried to ignore the discomfort.

Anna twirled her pen around on the paper. "Why are you using a burner phone? That's odd behavior."

"I lost my phone," he said, visibly calming himself. "Since I own a business, I had to quickly grab a disposable phone before driving here when Heather told me she needed help."

"I most certainly did not," Heather protested.

Anna cleared her throat. "What kind of business?"

"It's a restaurant," he said. "I own a chain of them."

"You'd think you could get a woman without stalking one," Anna mused thoughtfully.

Heather coughed to cover a chuckle. It was nice having a smart aleck for a lawyer.

Red slashed into Jack's handsome face. Or what Heather had once considered handsome. These days she liked a more rough and rugged look, for sure. "I'd watch the slanderous tone," Jack grunted.

"It's only slander if it isn't true," Anna said cheerfully.

The door opened, and the sheriff poked his head inside. "Have you folks handled this?"

Anna tilted her head.

"It doesn't look like it," Jack muttered.

Anna sighed. "All right. Sheriff? We're going to need a copy of the video from this meeting, and my client would like to press charges against Jack for extortion." She clicked her pen closed. "Or blackmail. No, it's extortion. Attempted, anyway."

The sheriff sighed. "Maybe you all could drop all charges against each other so I can go back to hunting down meth heads and poachers?"

Heather stared right at Jack. "I'm in, if you are. We dismiss all complaints and say goodbye forever?" Yeah, she had him with the extortion claim. Darn, but Anna was a good lawyer. "It's your choice, Jack."

He pressed his lips together until they turned white. "I'll think about it."

Anna stood and handed over the crutches. "We'll give you twenty-four hours. Come on, Heather. We still have lunch to eat, right?"

CHAPTER 10

*D*arkness had fallen along with more snow as Quint strode up Heather's freshly shoveled walkway with Zena on his heels. He kicked a couple of ice chunks off the steps and then knocked on the door.

Anna opened it, munching on a piece of chicken. "Hey."

"Hey. Nice job with the walkway," he said, shrugging off his coat to hang in the alcove.

"Not my first snowstorm," she agreed, turning toward the living room.

Heather sat on the older sofa with her leg elevated on a pillow perched on the coffee table. "It was nice of you to do that, Anna." Then she reached out her arms as Zena jumped onto the sofa.

"Down, Zena," Quint barked.

Zena dropped her butt to the floor.

Heather's bottom lip popped out just enough to be freaking adorable. "She can come up here."

"No. She can't," Quint said as gently as he could. He had to keep the canine disciplined in order for her to do the job she needed to do.

"Are you hungry?" Anna asked.

Quint couldn't get rid of the itch between his shoulder blades. "No, but thanks. I've interviewed everyone even remotely located around the motel, and nobody has a clue who the vandal was last night. According to the clerk, Jack arrived by himself and hasn't been seen with a woman."

Heather sat straighter, her legs encased in yoga pants and a light pink sweatshirt covering her ample chest. She kind of matched the Christmas tree, but Quint knew better than to say that. "You've been working on my case?"

"Yeah, but I didn't get any results." He dropped into the matching chair by the fireplace.

Anna finished her chicken and walked toward her boots by the door. "We'll see what we can discover tomorrow. If nothing else, I made sure Jack knew that if he didn't withdraw his complaint, we'd file a report against him for extortion."

Heather rubbed her nose. "Isn't that extortion?"

Anna grinned. "Sure, but it's all in how you word it, and I didn't word it like he did. Dumbass." Her eyes sparkled. "I'll talk to you both tomorrow. My Nana O'Shea is waiting for me. Night." She disappeared into the snowy night.

Quint studied the quiet woman on the sofa. "How dangerous is this guy?"

"I'm not sure. He never seemed dangerous before, but it's weird that he followed me to Silverville and then set up that weird attack on his car. It had to be him, right?" She shifted her leg to the side and winced.

"Yeah," Quint murmured. "I think I should go talk to him."

One of her light eyebrows lifted in a way that made her look like a sexy librarian. "Why? You gonna beat him up?"

"If I have to," he acknowledged.

She grinned. "Don't be silly. You being charged with a battery is probably a bad idea. I can handle Jack—especially with my lawyer's help. Anna is really good."

"She's very good, but she has to get back to work, and somebody needs to talk to this Jack." Apparently that was Quint, and he was more than ready to have a word or two. "Come on, Zena." He stood and snapped his fingers at his dog.

"Hey." Heather struggled to stand and hopped toward him on one foot. "I said no."

He cocked his head and fought the urge to help her since her face was flushed and her pretty lips pursed. How mad was she? "I understand, but I don't think this guy is getting the message."

She hopped right up to him. "I'm not looking for a protector, Quintino."

"That's unfortunate, because it seems like you need one." He gave in and grasped her upper arms to help her keep balanced.

She glared, and then those light emerald eyes dropped their focus to his mouth.

Oh, shit. Heat ran through him, pooling low in his groin. This close, her intriguing scent of apple cider washed over him. "Heather."

"What?" She moved closer and tilted her head, studying his eyes.

"Have you been drinking?" His voice lowered a couple of octaves to a hoarse tenor.

Her smile was slow and way too dangerous. "Just one glass of wine, country boy. I know what I'm doing."

What the hell was she doing? He kept his hold gentle. "Want to explain?"

"Sure." She grasped his flanks and dug her fingers into his ribs. "I had an epiphany earlier today. You know? A climax?"

Oh sweet lord. She was messing with him on purpose. "I know what an epiphany is, darlin'."

"That's good." She settled even closer, keeping her injured ankle lifted. "Life is short and unexpected. I've chosen wrong before, and I'm not looking for forever." She caressed around to his abs and up his chest. "I like you."

His zipper cut into his cock. "I like you, too." His mind reeled and he tried to find some sense of logic. *Any* sense of logic. "I thought we agreed this was a bad idea."

"The mere idea that we had to find an agreement shows that there's something here to explore," she whispered, leaning up to kiss beneath his jaw. The feeling shot right to his groin, and his heartbeat started thundering against his breastbone. "Unless you don't want me."

Desire tightened every muscle in his body. "You know I want you." It was impossible not to want her.

She lifted her hands to his shoulders. "All right, then." With that statement, she jumped from one foot.

* * *

HEATHER HAD a second to question her sanity before Quint caught her in the air and took her mouth. Hard. She'd thought about him all day and couldn't get rid of the thought that he'd carried her down a mountain. He was strong and sweet and nicely over-protective.

Oh, she knew he didn't want anything serious right now, and that was fine.

Right now, she just wanted him. So she kissed him back, knowing he'd keep her from falling.

He released her mouth, and his eyes had darkened. "Is this because you're scared? I'm not going to let anything happen to you. I promise."

"I'm not scared," she whispered against his mouth. She wasn't. Jack was a jerk and apparently a manipulative jackass, but she wasn't frightened of him. He'd pretty much backed down after Anna threatened him, and soon he'd have to leave town and go back to work. "This is about you and me. No pressure."

"No pressure." Quint kissed her again, his hands holding her aloft by the butt, his chest firm against her front. He turned and carried her toward her bedroom, and his tongue swept inside her mouth to take. He tasted like flavored coffee and mint, and she wanted more.

A lot more.

"Careful of your ankle." He set her on the bed and gently lifted her shirt over her head. "I've wanted to do that since I first saw you on the mountain." His large hands dropped to her full breasts.

Heat lashed through her, and she swayed toward him.

"Are you sure?" he rumbled, dropping to his knees in front of her.

"Yes," she whispered, tangling her fingers in his thick hair. "Definitely sure."

His smile was a little wicked and a lot heated. "All right." With a flick of his fingers, the front clasp of her bra sprang open. The sound he made was one she'd remember for the rest of her life. Male and hungry. He smelled like the forest, fir and pine, and the wild. His mouth found her breast, and she gasped.

So good and so fast.

"Careful now," he said against her, his thumbs tucking into her yoga pants. "Watch your ankle." Then he slowly, tortuously, drew the yoga pants off, his fingers infinitely gentle near her damaged ankle and cast. "If anything starts to hurt, you tell me." He leaned down and kissed her knee.

At the moment, she had all sorts of aches.

So she grasped his hair and tugged him closer, her mouth seeking his.

He let her kiss him and slowly took over, lifting her up farther on the bed. She yanked on his shirt and forced him to duck his head to let her throw the material out of the way. Then she finally felt that amazing chest. Skin on skin this time. Hard muscle, smooth lines, powerful strength. Yeah. She sighed. Then she leaned up to kiss him again.

His talented fingers tangled in the hair at her nape, and he pulled her head back. "Sweetheart? Here, I'm in charge." Then he kissed her again, going deep and destroying any argument, even if she'd been able to find one.

His hand swept down her body, marking her curves and leaving an imprint of him wherever he touched. The thought hit her that she couldn't keep this casual, but he kissed his way between her breasts and down her body, and it was too late.

Way too late.

He nipped her thigh before turning his head. His mouth found her, right where she wanted him, and she fell back onto the pillow as sensations overtook her. So many and so fast. The first orgasm slammed through her with the force of a winter storm. The second swept her out of her own mind, and the third had her whimpering his name.

Then, and only then, did he remove his jeans and lever over her after finding a condom in his wallet. Slowly, carefully, he powered inside her.

Her gaze met his and vulnerability swam through her.

He kissed her again, this time with a gentleness she felt throughout her entire body. "Quint," she murmured.

"I'm here. Right with you," he murmured, somehow knowing just what to say. He kept moving and finally embedded himself fully inside her. There was a lot to Quint Albertini, without question.

She tried to lift her knees to the sides of his hips, and he stopped her with a strong hand on her thigh.

"Your ankle. Keep your leg still," he said, holding her leg down.

Desire burst through her again, even stronger than before.

"There you go." He started to move, to hammer inside her, to take all of her.

She could only close her eyes and hold on, letting the tumultuous sensations take her away. For so long, he kept her at the edge, his stamina incredible. He sped up, pistoning inside her even harder, and she broke. The room flashed hot and then white, and she cried out his name, digging her nails into his arms.

He grunted her name as his body shuddered with his own release.

She tried to catch her breath, and her mind spun. Slowly, she withdrew her nails from his skin. He kissed her on the nose and slid out of her, heading to the bathroom to take care of the condom. When he returned, he lifted her and put them both beneath the covers.

"Are you all right?" He spooned around her and nipped the top of her ear.

"Yes." But was she? Everything inside her was relaxed, satiated, and off kilter. She wanted more of him. Yeah, she wanted all of him.

He kissed her ear again. "Good. Get some sleep." His phone buzzed, and he stiffened behind her. "Hold on." He released her and rummaged around on the floor. "Yeah. Albertini," he answered. The atmosphere in the room became heavy. "Understood. I'll be there." He clicked off and snuggled back around her.

She blinked and couldn't help cuddling her butt closer to his groin. "Be where?"

"Fire in Montana," he murmured against her head. "I have to leave first thing in the morning."

She frowned. "Fire in December? That's rare, right?"

"Yep." He flattened his hand over her abdomen. "We had a dry spring, hot summer, and a very late winter. Lightning strikes can cause problems, and we have a forest fire. The good news is that it should really start snowing soon, so we might not have to fight it for long."

Great. The guy she'd just figured out she was probably falling for was about to parachute into a wildfire caused by lightning.

She was such a moron sometimes.

$\mathcal{A}$nna showed up in the morning with lattes. Snow clung to her lashes as she stepped inside the front door and handed one to Heather. "Hey. I have a plan in mind." She paused at seeing the dog sleeping on the floor near the sofa. "Oh." A light crimson filtered across her cheekbones. "Um, okay. Why don't you call me later?"

Heather pulled her inside. "Quint isn't here. He left early in the morning to handle a fire in Montana."

Anna stiffened. "I've heard they've had a dry autumn and late winter snowfall over there, so I shouldn't be surprised. But I still worry when he heads off to parachute." She shuffled her feet. "He left his dog here this morning?" She pressed her lips together.

Heather rolled her eyes. "Yes, okay? We're grownups and all of that." She banished thoughts of wildfires and what could go wrong with parachutes. Then she caught sight of the dark circles beneath Anna's eyes. "Are you all right?"

"Yes." Anna took a deep gulp of her coffee. "I staked out Jack's motel room last night because I figured he'd need to meet with the person he hired to impersonate you, and nobody showed up. I thought you might like to tail him with me today. I have Nonna

Albertini on him right now, but she'll probably try to interrogate him with a wooden spoon to the head, so we should take her place."

Heather jerked. Wooden spoon? "Yeah, let's go." It was better than just sitting in her house worrying about Quint. "Can Zena come?"

The dog lifted her head.

"Always," Anna said. "Come on, girl."

The dog bounded across the room and licked Anna's hand before running outside to take care of business in the snow.

Heather drew on her jacket and hobbled on the crutches outside and down the porch to the walkway, which Quint had shoveled that morning before leaving. The snow continued to fall, however. Slow and soft this morning.

Anna opened the passenger side door of a black Ford truck. "I usually drive a Fiat, but it had some trouble earlier this year and I prefer Aiden's truck on the snow." She helped Heather inside and tossed the crutches in the back seat before the dog leaped inside. "Settle down, Zena. Good girl." Then she crossed around and lifted herself up into the truck. "Did Quint feed Zena before leaving?"

"Yeah," Heather said. "He left the whole bag in my kitchen and asked if I'd keep her while he was gone. It's nice to have the company."

Anna nodded. "I agree. Zena is wonderful to have around. Both Aiden and I have hectic schedules, so we just can't take care of an animal right now. Sometimes I borrow Zena, and I know Aiden likes her, too."

"Aiden seems like a nice boyfriend," Heather said, curious about the couple.

Anna ignited the engine and drove down the icy road. She winced.

Heather bit her lip. "Sorry. Was that a bad thing to say?" Maybe they were having problems.

"No." Anna chuckled. "It's just that the word 'boyfriend' doesn't fit Aiden, you know? He's a badass and I can't figure out what to call him. Friend, partner, or lover all sound wrong, too."

Heather held her hands closer to the heat bursting from the vents. "How about *your* 'badass?'"

Anna turned down another road through town. "That's better than 'boyfriend,' but it's still a little off. I'm not sure. Either way, he's my *something*."

Quint didn't seem like a 'boyfriend,' either. Not that it mattered. Last night was just last night, although the imprint of his teeth was still on Heather's left buttock. She hid her smile behind her latte cup and took a drink. It took her a second to realize she was softly humming Christmas songs.

Anna slid on the icy road and then corrected. "You're in a good mood."

"I don't want to talk about it," Heather said, unable to hold back the smile.

Anna shrugged. "It's your choice, but you and Quint seem like a good match, at least to me." She slowed down to let a couple of fawns run across the road up ahead. "So long as you can deal with his job and understand it's part of him. He'll always want to be front and center with saving people and risking himself to do it."

Could Heather handle that? Was she strong enough? "Chrissy seemed like a nice person, but she couldn't deal with his job?" Not that it was Heather's business.

"No. She was needy and always calling him for reassurance, and I think when he's on a job, he has to concentrate solely on that job." Anna glanced toward Heather. "Probably like you when you write and illustrate a story. I imagine you get lost in another world."

That was an excellent way to put it. Although, friend zone? Heather turned toward her new friend. "I'm not sure about anything right now. I'm just getting settled in town, have an ex stalking me, and have the law waiting to arrest me. Quint was clear that he just wanted to be friends—albeit with benefits—so talking about anything more is just fantasizing." But after one night with him, she had a lot to fantasize about. Quintino Albertini knew how to kiss…as well as do everything else.

Heat filtered through her body.

Anna drove to the far end of the parking lot to Molly's Motel, which was just off I-90. "Anyway, no matter what happens, I'm glad we've become friends."

"Me, too," Heather said, settling comfortably into the heated leather seat. She had friends already. Life was definitely looking up.

The motel was painted a bright red and white, and cheerful blue Christmas bulbs lined every eve. A larger than life blown up Santa stood by the main door, his hat covered with real snow and icicles extending from his arms and wide nose.

"Jack is in room 12 on the first floor." Anna pointed.

"I recognize his car out front." Heather took another sip and studied the snow-covered SUV that now had key marks and dents all over the metal.

A maroon-colored Buick fired up at the other end of the parking lot and drove their way, parking on Anna's side. The window rolled down to reveal Nonna Albertini with her hair in a scarf, and her eyes covered by wide Audrey-Hepburn style sunglasses. "The perp hasn't moved an inch," she whispered.

Anna leaned out the window. "Tell me you aren't wearing a trench coat."

"It's your grandfather's," Nonna confirmed. "I say we make things happen here. How about I roust him out of the room and you two follow him?"

Heather's mouth gaped open.

Anna somehow managed to keep a straight face. "I think we'll do this the old-fashioned way, Nonna. You go on home, and we'll just watch and see what Jack does. If we need backup, I promise you're the first person we'll call."

Her grandmother's eyebrow rose. "Are you armed? If not, I brought the Glock."

"I'm armed. My Smith and Wesson is in the glovebox," Anna said.

"Don't be afraid to use it." Her Nonna dug around in a monstrous purse and handed up a wooden spoon. "This is an extra weapon. Just in case you don't need bullets."

Anna dutifully accepted the spoon. "You're the best. Thanks."

"Any time. You girls be careful." The window rolled up, and Nonna drove sedately out of the parking lot to the quiet road.

Anna set the spoon on the seat between them. "See why I wanted to hurry?"

Heather burst out laughing, unable to help herself. "I love her. The woman looks just like Sophia Loren, don't you think?"

Anna grinned. "Yeah. She hears that a lot." She kicked her legs out. "Her idea wasn't bad. What do you think about dealing with this head-on?"

Heather finished her coffee. "I'm all for it. I think I should go talk to him alone and see if I can get him to confess everything." She'd been thinking about the situation all morning. "If he can be a manipulative jackass, I don't see why I can't do the same thing." She dug her phone from her purse. "I'll set the phone to record and see what I can find out."

Anna nodded. "Agreed." She pushed the spoon toward Heather. "Take the spoon. You'd be surprised how effective it can be when smacked against somebody's nose."

Heather shoved the spoon in her purse. "Do you mind driving closer?" Ice covered the cemented parking area, and she'd no doubt fall on the crutches.

"No problem. I'm going to park right outside, and if you scream, I'll come running. Armed," Anna said, driving across the lot to park next to Jack's SUV. "You can do this."

Adrenaline heated Heather's veins, and her breath panted, but she forced herself to remain calm. "Yep. No problem."

Zena whined from the back seat and lifted her head. Her soft brown eyes seemed to provide a warning.

"You could take the dog," Anna mused. "If Jack does try anything, Zena can be fierce."

"Good idea." While Heather wanted to get to the bottom of the situation and find out who Jack had hired to impersonate her, she wasn't stupid. He was obviously a little nutty, and having a dog protecting her was just smart. "What do you think, Zena? Are you up for a job?"

The dog barked and sat up.

"There you go," Anna said.

Heather hauled the crutches over the seat and opened her door, gingerly stepping out. She started recording on her phone and slipped it into her coat pocket with the speaker barely poking out. "Come on, girl."

Zena bounded over the seat and jumped outside, sliding across the ice.

Heather drew her shoulders tight and hitched across the ice to knock on Jack's door.

He opened it wearing tan pants with a blue sweater, having obviously shaved and showered already. He backed up a step. "Heather." Pleasure warmed his eyes.

"I thought we should talk." She moved inside along with the dog.

He glanced down at the canine. "You didn't need to bring protection. I'd never hurt you." He frowned, his wide hand still on the doorway. "You have to know that."

Her head jerked back as her body recoiled. "You tried to have me arrested for vandalism. You set me up. That's hurtful."

He shook his head and gestured her inside. "I did no such thing."

She looked around to see a king-sized bed, two chairs by a table, and an older television set on a credenza. The curtains were open, and the snowy day brought brightness inside. It was time to manipulate him. "If we're going to get through this, you need to be honest with me." She sat gingerly in one of the chairs, careful to keep her pocket pointed toward him.

He shut the door and sat in the other chair. "I am being honest." His earnest expression was going to get him smacked with a wooden spoon.

Zena growled and moved to sit by Heather's foot. "Even the dog doesn't believe you, Jack."

Jack reached to take her hand and drew back when she glared. "I don't understand why you damaged my car after I sent you roses. Obviously you need help, and I want to provide that. Please let me."

Did the guy know he was being recorded? Or was he so crazy that he'd actually convinced himself that he hadn't hired somebody to impersonate her—crutches and all? "I don't need help, but I'm thinking you do." She kept her purse close in case she needed to clock him. "When I broke up with you, I meant it."

"Your grandmother died and you need somebody to be here for you," he said gently. "I know we broke up, but after you keyed my car the other night, I understand that you require more assistance than I'd thought. We meant something to each other, and I want to help you. Come away with me to the cabin. It's peaceful and restful there, and you can regain your equilibrium."

"As you chain me to the wall," she snapped. "You really need to listen and get this through your thick head. I do not want to date you, see you, or talk to you. Please just leave me alone."

His lips turned down. "I can see that you're refusing to be rational. There's nothing I can do, then. Pay for the damages to my car, and I'll leave town."

Oh, he did not. She shook her head as the hair rose along Zena's back. How had she missed that he was nuts? "No."

He sighed. "Then I'm going to press charges. Either you let me help you, or I'll make sure the system does."

What a complete ass. She stood and placed her crutches

beneath her arms. "Fine. I'll press charges, too. This town is small enough that we will find who you hired to beat up your car. It's only a matter of time." She began to move toward the door, and he stood, blocking her way.

Awareness ticked down her spine. She'd forgotten how tall he was this close. "What are you doing?"

"Trying to save you from yourself," he grit out, his teeth clenching.

Zena growled and stood between them, and Heather scrambled inside her purse, brandishing the wooden spoon. "Get out of my way."

He blinked. "That's a wooden spoon."

She nodded. "Move, Jack."

The door burst open, right into him, and he crashed into the credenza. Anna stood there, gun in hand. "I saw you go for the spoon through the window."

Heather looked down at Jack, who was bleeding from the temple and glaring at them both. Her spine straightened and her stomach stopped cramping. "Nice hit."

CHAPTER 12

$\mathcal{H}$e'd been away from home for three days, and this was the first time he wanted to hurry back in a long time. After his shower in the antiquated motel bathroom, Quint slipped on sweats and an old T-shirt. His body hurt, and a slight burn on his wrist was driving him nuts. But it had been a successful jump, and this time he even had his own room in the closest crappy motel since the fire was pretty much out now. Oh, it'd smolder for a little while, but dealing with that wasn't his job.

Unfortunately, finding dead bodies was his job. If he'd known the fire would be that easy to quench in three days, he would've brought Zena with him. Of course, he hadn't expected the strong snowstorm that had unexpectedly arrived.

He sat on the flowered bedspread and sent a video-call to Heather. He hadn't had a chance to call before now because he'd stayed in a tent closer to the national forest and hadn't had any service. It was surprising how badly he wanted to see her face and hear her voice. Not that he'd share that fact with anyone.

She answered from her kitchen. "Hi."

"Hi." Everything inside him settled at seeing her pretty face. "What are you doing?"

"Baking cookies to thank Anna for being my lawyer." Heather pushed a wayward blonde curl out of her eyes. "How are you?"

He took in her sparkling eyes. "I'm fine. The fire is almost out, so it's going to be a quicker trip than I expected. How's my dog?"

"Fine. She's tough," Heather said, looking down and to the side. "I made her some doggie treats that she likes, and I hope that's okay." She leaned down, obviously petting the dog. "Are you headed home tonight or do you have to wait a couple of days?"

Was it wishful thinking, or did she sound hopeful? He rubbed his chest. Oh, he was getting in too deep too fast. "I'll be a few more days, and I'm trying to get ahold of Anna to have her bring Zena over." Usually one of his brothers helped him out, but they were all swamped. "Maybe the two of you can come." Why did he say that? The last thing he wanted was for Heather to see him at his darkest. She was a softie, and she deserved the home-bound, fun-loving Quint.

Her teeth played with her bottom lip.

He'd already fantasized enough about that mouth the night before, and he had to shove down a groan.

She smiled. "How about I bring Zena over? Anna returned to work for some important case about a rogue Santa. I don't have more details than that."

That sounded like his cousin. He sighed. "Are you sure? It's a drive even without an injured ankle."

"I can drive," she said, her face lighting up. "My good ankle and foot are what I use for the gas pedal and braking. Zena and I would love to get out of here and see you. I mean, if you want."

The hesitation in her voice did him in. "Of course I want to see you. Just be careful on the drive." Wait a minute. "Why do you need to get out of there?"

She rolled her eyes and filled him in on the situation with Jack at his motel a few days ago. By the end, his ears were hot.

Quint swallowed. "How about you, Anna, and Nonna leave the investigations to the police?" What in the world had they been

85

thinking? At least they'd had the good sense to take Zena with them.

"We decided the same thing," Heather said, her cheek creasing. "Although you should've seen Jack's face when he hit the credenza. He's going forward with the vandalism charges, though. I wish he'd just leave town."

If not, Quint would take that time to have a talk with the man. It was time. So getting Heather out of town was actually a good idea. "Okay. Please wait until it's light outside tomorrow morning before heading this way. I'll text you directions, and you text me when you leave the house." They'd need to check in every hour, but he would be out at the fire for some of the time. "Are you sure you want to do this?"

"Of course."

He settled back on the bed. "All righty, then. So. Want to talk dirty?"

Her face cleared, and then a soft blush filled her cheeks. "I've, um, never done that."

He grinned at the interest in her green eyes. "Let me show you." Then he relaxed and eased her into goofing off with him long distance.

The woman was a fast learner.

* * *

THE MORNING BROUGHT heavy snow and freezing rain. Heather made sure Zena was comfortable in the back seat of her SUV and then settled herself into the driver's seat with her crutches next to her. It was only a four-hour drive, mostly on I-90, which should be plowed already. "Let's do this, puppy." She slowly drove onto the icy road and headed through town and to I-90.

Quint called every hour to check on her, and by the time she pulled into the parking lot at his lonely side-of-the-road motel, she had decided the friend zone sucked. In fact, there was no way she wanted to keep him there.

He met her, dressed in jeans and a thick T-shirt with a slight burn down the side of his neck. His dark hair was back from his face, his brown eyes were soft at seeing her, and a dangerous looking scruff covered his jaw. Everything inside her went all gooey when he opened her car door. "Hi."

"Hi." She stood and was careful to keep her balance on one foot. A slight smoke fog still hung in the frozen air. "I missed you." Crap. Why had she said that?

He ran his knuckles down the side of her face. "I missed you, too."

Okay. That was good. Then she caught the shadows in his eyes. "Is everything okay?"

He whistled for the dog. "Yeah. We just have a job to do. There are at least three missing hikers in the fire area, and there's no way they made it out." Zena jumped out the front door and immediately ran over to an ice covered bush to take care of business. "I'm not usually in a decent mood afterward."

"I wouldn't expect you to be," she murmured. Had everyone put pressure on him to wear a bright face when he was dealing with death? "Just be you, Quint." She couldn't say it any clearer than that.

He paused and looked at her. Really looked at her. "Are you sure?"

"Yes." She patted his strong chest. "Be as quiet or cranky as you want. I'll give you the space."

Something shifted in his eyes. She wasn't sure what, but it felt like something big. He took her hand and led her inside a shabby but clean looking motel room. "I'll get your bag."

She looked around while he fetched her bag from the car. The shag carpet had seen better days, but a window out the back showed snow-covered trees and a chilly looking river. The sound was soothing and would help her write while she waited for him.

He set her belongings by the door. "I, ah, should've asked if you wanted two rooms. We should only be here a day or two. Tops."

After phone sex? She faced him head-on. "I want one room."

His grin was slow and way too sensual. "Me, too." A truck rumbled to a stop outside, and he glanced over his shoulder. "That's my ride. I left the menu from the pizza place—the only one around here—by the door. Just order whatever you want. Zena and I will be back right after dark." Then, he hesitated only briefly before stalking across the room and planting a hard one on her mouth.

She grinned. "Be careful."

"You, too," he murmured, kissing her again and then turning for the doorway. He grabbed his jacket off the lumpy looking bed and shut the door on the storm.

She touched her lips in the sudden silence. Well, except for the rushing river. Sighing, she hobbled to her bag and removed her laptop to write and match some of the illustrations she'd created the last few days. The table by the back window was solid, and she worked away, trying to keep her mind off Quint and Zena and what a rough afternoon they were probably having.

When darkness began to arrive, she ordered pizza, already starving. There was a small fridge beneath the television set, so she could save plenty for Quint.

A knock sounded on the door and she grasped her purse, hopping to open the door. A second too late, she caught her mistake when she sighted the man standing there. "Jack."

"You're in danger." He pushed her back and slammed the door, rushing over to the window and peeking out the blinds. A bandage covered his temple from his injury the other day. "You were followed. How could you not have noticed?" He looked over his shoulder, his eyes wild. "This is crazy. I mean, the whole situation is nuts. We have to go out the back."

Her mouth went dry. "It's okay," she croaked. Just how delusional was he? "How about we go out the front?"

"No." He pushed past her toward the rear windows. "These are big enough. We can just get through. I'll carry you. It's okay." His fingers fumbled, but he managed to shove the frozen window to the side. "Come on, Heather. Now. Let's go." A knife handle stuck out of his pocket.

Her gaze dropped to the weapon. She could go out the front door, but with her crutches, she might not get far. Of course, she could scream for help, but if the motel was occupied only by the firefighters, they'd all be gone. Perhaps there was somebody in the office. She could scream that loud.

"Heather. Now." His dilated gaze tracked her and he lumbered across the shag carpet to grab her arm.

She patted his elbow. There had to be a way to get out of this. "All right, Jack. Take a deep breath. You're the only one who followed me." She kept her voice as calm and soothing as she could considering the lump that was in her throat. Could she get the knife from him? "I'm going to get you help."

He manacled both her arms and shook her. "Listen to me. I saw you get on the interstate and then a car followed you. I followed it, and we all ended up here. All day I've been waiting for your stalker to make a move, and now that it's getting dark, we have to get out of here. Please trust me. Let's go."

"You're whack-a-doodle, Jack." She jerked free. How had she not seen him behind her? She'd checked several times. "Nobody followed me but you."

The door shoved open. "Well, that's not exactly true."

Heather jolted as her mind fought to catch up with her sight. "Chrissy?" The woman stood in the doorway with a very shiny silver gun pointed right at Heather's chest.

CHAPTER 13

"*B*ack up." Chrissy motioned with the gun, reaching behind herself with her free hand to lock the door.

Heather hopped back to sit on the bed, her mind spinning.

Jack sighed, dropped his hands, and moved to sit by her. "I told you."

Chrissy was dressed in curvy jeans, a pastel sweater, and topaz jewelry. She shut the door and leaned back against it, her eyes hard. "I wanted to wait until Quint returned to have this discussion, but your buddy here ruined that idea. So I guess we figure this out together."

Heather tried to listen for any movement outside, but only the river echoed back. "What's going on, Chrissy?" Did she have a chance to calm the woman?

Chrissy pointed the gun at Heather's face.

Heather winced and fought the need to cover her head. Her hands shook around her purse. "Don't shoot me. Just hold on a minute."

"Don't ask me for favors," the woman spat. "Everything was getting better until you showed up. How *dare* you come to the family barbecue!"

All right. Batshit crazy town. Heather swallowed. "I thought you were dating Trick."

"Ha. He was just my way to get back to the family and to Quint. We're meant to be together. He's mine." Red flushed ugly from Chrissy's neck to her forehead, making her eyes bulge. "I had a plan, and then you went and got stuck on a mountain. Quint's a fucking hero, and once he became that to you, he was all in."

Heather turned her head. "Jack? Why didn't you just call the police if you knew I was being followed?"

His gaze remained on the barrel of the gun. "I wanted to be your hero. Figured if I helped you out of here, that you'd want to come to the cabin with me." Then his attention turned to Chrissy's curvy form. "Wait a minute."

Her smile rivaled a cat's. "Yeah. I keyed your car. I had crutches from an injury years ago and thought I could hide my face well enough. I figured Heather would look like a psycho and Quint would drop her instantly." Her hand shook on the gun. "But that didn't happen, did it?"

Jack cleared his throat. "I thought she was nuts."

Chrissy's nostrils flared. "Quint didn't. In fact, he stayed the night at your house, didn't he, Heather? I watched his truck all night, and he stayed with you." Her voice rose to shrill at the end of the sentence.

Heather winced. "I didn't know you two were still together."

"We are," Chrissy snapped. "We just had a bump in the road, but as soon as I get pregnant, he'll find a different job in town. Then everything will be all right."

Now that was a plan. Heather shook her head. "How did you follow me without my knowing?"

Chrissy set her stance. "Oh, please. When Quint left his dog at your house, I knew you'd be bringing her to the fire. So I tagged your car. It's easy to do. I've had a tracker on his for a year."

Jack subtly moved closer to the edge of the bed. "How did you know I was in town to see Heather? And how did you know to key my car?"

"It's Silverville and there are no secrets," Chrissy said, turning the gun toward him. "Back on the bed, buddy."

He scooted back.

Heather sucked in air as the last week ran through her mind. "Did you shoot at Quint the other night?"

"Of course not. He's going to be the father of my children," Chrissy said, her voice almost girly now. "I shot at that bitch Jolene. How dare she show up at his house. I was going to knock on his door after having had a fight with Trick, and then we would've gotten back together. Jolene deserved to get shot. So do you."

Chills clattered down Heather's back. For the first time since getting her cast, she actually felt vulnerable. Not strong. But she could still fight, and she still had her brain. "Quint won't like it if you shoot us."

Chrissy smiled. "He's not going to know it was me, silly."

Jack sucked in air. "You can't just kill us."

"Sure, I can." Chrissy tilted her head, and her gaze ran over his body. "You're a good looking guy, Jack-Jack. Why are you chasing this piece of fluff all over the state?"

Jack's fingers curled into the tattered bedspread. "I thought we were in love."

Chrissy snorted. "Obviously not. You should've worked harder at keeping her. Just think how much better off we all would be right now?"

Heather pressed her good foot to the floor. "You can't shoot us and leave us here for Quint to find. You'd be an instant suspect."

"Maybe, maybe not," Chrissy said, fluttering her eyelashes and then widening her eyes. "Either way, I'm just shooting Jack and taking you with me, so they'll think you did it. They'll never find your body."

Jack tensed. "Then you'll comfort Quint. It's not a bad plan."

"Thanks." Chrissy preened. Then she sobered. "I'm really sorry you got caught up in this."

"Me too." Jack held his breath.

"Now!" Heather pulled the wooden spoon from the purse, ducked her head, and pushed off with her good foot, aiming for Chrissy's midsection.

The firing of the gun was thunderous.

* * *

QUINT HAD ALMOST REACHED his motel room door when gunfire stopped him cold. "Heather?" He viciously twisted the knob and smashed into the door, bouncing back. It was locked?

Heather screamed inside.

Panic seized him. He threw his shoulder into the wood, and the door flew open, cracking down the middle. Charging inside, he jumped Heather's crutches to see Heather and Chrissy grappling on the floor, a gun flashing around.

Jack Allen lay on the bed with blood on his face. His eyes were closed.

The gun fired and a bullet whizzed by Quint's ear. "Shit." He ducked low, trying to keep an eye on the gun.

Heather wildly smacked Chrissy with a wooden spoon, grunting as she moved to the side to avoid the gun. The clap of the spoon competed with the shrieking of the two women.

Chrissy screamed and fired again. The bullet smashed through the window, shattering glass in every direction as the curtains dropped to the antiquated heater.

Zena barked wildly from the doorway.

Shards of glass ripped into the back of Quint's neck. In a second, everything became clear to him. He caught sight of the gun and went in fast, sliding on his knees and ripping it free of Chrissy's hand. In one smooth motion, he shoved the gun in the back of his waist and captured Heather around the waist.

He twisted and put her behind him.

Chrissy looked up, a welt beneath her eye. "Quint. You're here. I'm so glad. She attacked me."

Quint took a deep breath. He had the gun and Heather was safe. "What in the hell is happening?"

Tears filled Chrissy's eyes. "Please help me. They kidnapped me and brought me here. I barely got the gun away from that man. I'm so scared, Quint. Help."

Heather growled. "She's crazy. They both followed me, and then she shot Jack. She's also the one who damaged his car. The chick is all *Fatal Attraction* over you." She gasped in air, wheezing. "She also punched me in the gut."

Chrissy shook her head. "She's lying. I'm telling the truth. Please, Quint. Help me."

He couldn't believe he'd never really seen her before. "Did you shoot at me the other night?"

"No." Tears slid along Chrissy's face to fall toward her ears. "I was aiming at Jolene. She wanted to hurt you and your family. I'm just trying to protect you. You're my future."

The woman was nuts. Quint clamped her arms and flipped her onto her stomach. "Heather? Are you all right?" He tore his belt free and secured Chrissy's hands behind her back.

"Yes," Heather breathed, hopping to the bed. "Jack?"

Chrissy struggled, her face buried in the thick shag carpet. "Quint. Stop it."

Quint finished with the belt and stood, turning toward the bed.

Jack blinked awake and slowly sat up, gingerly touching his nose. "What the hell?"

Heather fell onto the side of the bed. "I think I elbowed you when I charged Chrissy."

Jack prodded his nose and then wiped blood off his face with his arm.

Quint settled as he scouted the room for any more threats. "You weren't shot?"

Jack looked down his body. "Um, no." He angled his head to see Chrissy writhing on the floor. "I'm not sure what happened. One second she was going to shoot us, and the next..."

Quint focused on Heather, heated energy roiling through him. "You charged a psycho with a gun—using a wooden spoon."

Heather's hand shook as she pushed hair out of her face. A bruise was already forming near her chin. "She was going to shoot us, so the risk seemed worth it." The color slowly slid out of her face.

Quint pulled his phone from his back pocket and dialed 9-1-1. He ended the call. "Heather. Here." At the moment, he wasn't capable of more words. He'd gone cold the second he'd heard the first shot.

She moved from the bed and hopped toward him.

The second she was within reach, he pulled her into his side. The world settled. "Are you sure you're all right?"

"Yes." She snuggled right in, tremors shaking through her body.

Jack watched him. "I think I'm due an apology here."

Quint sliced him with a look. "Really? You owe Heather an apology for filing vandalism charges. She told you it wasn't her." He made sure to keep Jack's gaze. "She's mine, buddy. We might as well get that straight right now."

Heather shifted slightly against him.

He kissed the top of her head, keeping her right where he wanted her. "We can argue about the arcane language later, darlin'." For now, he needed Jack to get him. "Are we clear?"

Jack slowly nodded, still holding his nose. "Yeah. We're clear." Truth be told, the guy looked a little relieved.

Chrissy started to roll over, and Heather dropped her casted foot onto her ass. "Stay still," Heather said.

Quint fought a grin. "You're something, sweetheart." Oh, it was

95

way too early to be thinking about the future, but everything inside him knew she'd be there. He'd give her time to get used to the idea, however.

She sighed and buried her face in his side. "It's been a rough day." Then she lifted up as sirens trilled outside. "But I'd take any day with you, Quintino Albertini."

He leaned down and kissed her nose. "Ditto."

Chrissy screamed into the carpet, and Jack made a gagging noise.

The sirens grew louder and closer.

Zena barked, long and loud.

Heather jolted and tried to pull away.

"Too late, darlin'," Quint said, meaning every word. "I'm keeping you."

CHAPTER 14

$\mathcal{H}$eather blushed as Quint's Nonna fussed over her, bringing yet another glass of wine. She sat up on the deck beneath a toasty heater as the snow lightly fell onto the river. The family was spread out over the deck, inside, and beneath heaters closer to the tree line for their weekly barbecue. "Thank you," she murmured, her body already nicely numb from wine.

"You're welcome." Nonna patted her head. "You were such a brave girl to take care of that nasty Chrissy. You know, I never liked that girl." She clicked her tongue and shook her head.

"Me either," Heather agreed, lifting the wine glass.

"I do like you, though." Nonna leaned in. "After we staked out that motel together, I started thinking about opening a detective agency. If you ever get tired of writing and illustrating, you give it some thought, no?"

"I'd love to," Heather said, wondering if the wine was affecting her judgment.

Nonna nodded. "Good girl. You keep that spoon I gave you, okay? You'll need it with our Quintino." She moved on with the wine bottle, pouring for people as she walked.

Quint returned from snatching another piece of the delicious apple pie. He sat next to her. "Are you sure you don't want anything else?"

She leaned against his side, trying to remember where she'd put that spoon. It was probably back in her purse. Something told her Quint wouldn't take to being smacked with it by her, however. Maybe she'd find out one day, but right now, he was just being too sweet. "I'm stuffed. You can stop babying me." She didn't mean it.

He took a large bite of the pie and chewed thoughtfully. "It's only been a few days since you charged a woman with a gun. Enjoy the babying while it lasts."

She had a feeling his protective nature might last forever, and she couldn't find fault with that. Even so, she didn't want to slide herself into a fantasy world like Chrissy had. "Any news on Chrissy?"

"Yeah. She's been charged in Montana, and I think they'll find her a nice looney bin for a while. She has family to help out, and the farther away I stay from her, the better." Quint's voice hardened just enough to go hoarse. "We're both going to stay away from her."

"No argument from me on that," Heather said easily. "I also heard from Jack. He's back home and said to tell you that he's never coming north again." For some reason, Jack had seemed frightened of Quint, which made no sense. They'd all been on the same side when Chrissy had gone crazy with the gun.

"Good," Quint said.

She looked at his assembled family, and one of his brothers winked at her. It'd take a while to learn everyone's names. She liked this group of people, and she felt at home with them. Even so, she didn't want to get ahead of herself. "Your family is acting like we're a couple."

"We are," he said simply, digging into the ice cream.

She turned to stare at his topaz eyes. "We are?"

He lifted one powerful shoulder, his gaze keeping hers. "Yeah.

Oh, you can take your time and we can date for as long as you want, but we're meant, Heather. My family usually senses when that happens." He grinned. "I'm a patient man."

A patient man who'd carried her down a mountain and then had charged into possible gunfire when he'd thought she was in danger. She smiled. "Maybe this was my plan the whole time."

"It's a good plan." He nodded at her wine glass. "Though don't get too fuzzy because I have plans for you tonight."

A thrill, the one she equated with Quint, shot through her. "Last night wasn't enough for you?"

"Nope." He finished off his pie and sat back, slinging an arm over her shoulders. "This morning was close, though." His grin turned wicked this time.

The shiver that took her had nothing to do with the falling snow and everything to do with the hottie Italian smokejumper holding her so close.

He kissed her nose and made her sigh.

Even so, if he was going to be so upfront, so was she. "It's way too early to say the *l* word," she murmured.

"Sure. Although you fell for me the second I saved your butt on the mountain." It probably wasn't arrogant if it was true.

She was too mellow to argue. "Maybe. Every girl wants a hero."

"Is that a fact?" He took a drink of her wine. "Well, you've got one if you want one."

"I want one," she whispered. "But just you. Not anyone." Her head was spinning a little, but she was safe with him. Completely. "You're the perfect hero for me." He and his rescue dog who'd found her on the mountain. Both of them had planted themselves squarely in her heart.

He kissed her then, on the deck with his family all around. Then he leaned back. "You're the perfect hero for me, too." Drawing her close, he tucked her right into his side, where he seemed to want her.

Forever.

EPILOGUE

*A*nna Albertini settled beneath the heater at her usual table with her sisters on either side of her drinking red wine. Pauley had chosen to eat inside at this barbecue, and she'd play a video game with him later. For now, the river rushed by, the heater kept them toasty, and family was all around. It was a good night, and everyone was safe.

For now, anyway.

Donna sipped the Chianti to her right, her boots covered in snow. "Think they'll have a spring or summer wedding?"

Anna studied Quint and Heather, noting how right they looked together. "Quint says he's patient, but he's really not."

Tessa sipped her Cabernet to Anna's left. "That's the truth. We're too close to Christmas right now. Does anybody know when Heather's birthday is? She seems like an Aquarius to me."

Donna snorted. "You already heard her tell Nonna that her birthday is in February. Don't act like you can guess a person's sign."

"I can," Tessa retorted. "It's a gift I get from the O'Shea side."

Anna took a deep drink of her Shiraz. "Regardless, February will be the perfect time to propose. They can have a summer wedding." Her heart warmed for her cousin. He deserved happiness and Heather was his perfect match. She could handle his job and the stress that came with it. "I wonder if she'll ask one of us to be in the wedding."

"Maybe," Tessa said. "At the very least, I'll bet she takes us dress shopping with her. She probably doesn't even know we have an aunt who owns a dress shop."

Donna leaned toward them. "Make sure Quint takes one of us ring shopping when he goes. He's a good guy, but he knows nothing about gems. He'll totally screw up the ring."

Anna nodded. "Yeah. You're not wrong. Remember that necklace he gave mom for her fiftieth birthday?"

They all shuddered.

"She still wears it when he's around, and the thing looks too heavy for her small neck," Donna laughed.

"His heart was in the right place," Tess chortled.

Anna's heart turned over as Aiden strode over to Quint and sat to chat. Speaking of being in the right place.

Donna nudged her. "I swear you look like one of those cartoon characters with hearts shooting out of their eyes. Try to play it a little cool."

"I am cool," Anna said, glancing at her phone. "But I need to get going soon. Work calls."

"Any interesting cases?" Tessa asked, watching Quint and Heather again.

Anna nodded. "Always. I'm defending Santa next week."

Donna jolted. "Of course you are."

Tessa erupted into peals of laughter.

Aiden looked their way, his gaze seeking Anna's. Once he saw her, he visibly relaxed. Yeah, she probably gave him plenty to worry about. She sighed. "Don't tell Aiden about Santa. He has enough going on right now."

Her sisters laughed harder.

Quint caught her gaze and lifted a wine glass in salute.

She smiled and lifted hers, whispering to her sisters. "The plan is working. So long as we keep the focus on the Albertini boys, Nonna and the aunts will leave us alone." So she could deal with work, Santa, and Aiden Devlin on her own with some breathing space.

Donna smiled. "Yep. One down and five to go. For now, let's just enjoy the happiness on Nonna's face."

Anna couldn't look away from Quint and Heather. They snuggled together in full view of the entire family. "You know, they really are."

"Are what?" Tessa asked.

Anna set down her wineglass. "Absolutely perfect for each other."

His cousin kissed the woman he loved again.

Yep. Just perfect.

SANTA'S SUBPOENA

AVAILABLE SEPTEMBER 28TH - SPECIAL PREORDER PRICE!

So Much for Peace During the Holidays!

Anna Albertini has her hands full during the holiday season. Her boyfriend Aiden is back in town after being undercover across the country for the last three months, and his sudden over-protectiveness is a little too much. In addition, Nonna's latest matchmaking scheme has been so far thwarted by the two most stubborn candidates alive, and Nonna is out of patience and bringing out the big guns. Anna is forced to both protect her sister and run interference, when she'd like to jump in and find a happily ever after for everyone instead.

To add to her already hectic life, her life-long stalker is about to make a move and doesn't hide that frightening fact, although Anna is more than ready for him. In fact, she's willing to draw him out to finally bring him down—regardless of the consequences. Finally, Santa has been arrested and charged for murder, needing a good lawyer. Who would arrest Santa? Anna can't let this stand. It's a good thing Christmas is a time of magic and miracles, because she's going to need one.

PURCHASE ORDER LINKS:

Santa's Subpoena

HOLIDAY ROGUE

CHECK OUT THE NEXT ALBERTINI HOLIDAY ROMANCE!

Danger and Mistletoe are a Deadly Combination

Bosco Albertini learned the hard way that focusing on his career is a lot safer than investing in love. So when he meets his sweet new neighbor, he puts her firmly in the friend zone, despite her soft hazel eyes, sharp wit, and tempting curves. It soon becomes difficult to keep her there because his brothers, his Nonna, and even his dog already adore her—and he's not far behind.

Marlie Kreuk accepts the friend zone from the too sexy soldier because, hey, when a guy puts you there, he's a moron who doesn't deserve more. But when danger comes for her and Bosco risks his spectacular body to protect her, she can't help but wish for romance. Although, he's going to have to work for it.

With danger all around, Bosco and Marlie must face their explosive attraction while defeating deadly attackers, but even that is nothing compared to handling the Albertini matchmakers during the Christmas season. Busting out of that friend zone and surviving will take all of Bosco's training, Marlie's courage, and the magic of the holidays.

PURCHASE LINKS:
Holiday Rogue

DISORDERLY CONDUCT CHAP. 1

TAKE A LOOK AT THE FIRST ANNA ALBERTINI NOVEL!

My latte tasted like it was missing the flavor. It might be because I had less than a week until I received an anniversary card from a sociopath, and the waiting was painful. Sighing, I took another sip. Well, the brew wasn't so bad, and the prosecuting attorney's office was fairly quiet this morning, so I could get caught up on paperwork.

The outside doors burst open, slamming loudly against the traditional oak paneling. What in the world? I jumped up and ran around my desk, skidding to a stop at my doorway to see a cluster of men stalk inside. Weapons were strapped to their thighs. Big ones.

It felt like a blitz attack.

The receptionist in the waiting area yelled, and a paralegal walking while reading a stack of papers stopped cold in spiked pumps, dropping the papers. Her name was Juliet, and I'd just met her last month but didn't know much about her except she liked to use colored paperclips when handing over case files.

She sidled closer to me; her eyes wide. Even though I wore thick wedges, she towered over me by about a head.

Six agents strode inside, all big and broad, all wearing blue jackets with yellow DEA letters across their backs. There should be a woman or three among them. Why just men? More importantly, why was the DEA invading the prosecuting attorney's offices?

The shortest agent slapped a piece of paper on the reception desk, and the other five stomped around her, prowling down the long hallways and past my office which was the nearest to the reception area. Being the most junior of all the deputy prosecutors, I was lucky to have an office, if it could be called such. I waited until the grim looking agents had passed before walking across the scattered papers to read what predictably turned out to be a warrant.

An arrest warrant.

I tried to digest that reality when the tallest agent, a guy with light blond hair and light-refracting glasses that concealed the color of his eyes, escorted Scot Peterson, the prosecuting attorney, out of the office in handcuffs. My boss was around sixty-something years old with thick salt and pepper hair, bright blue eyes, and a sharp intelligence that had won him cases at the Idaho Supreme Court on more occasions that I could count.

He didn't look right cuffed. I finally burst out of the fuzz of shock, and heat slammed through me. What was happening? Scot was a decent guy. He helped people and even taught for free at the local community college. The agent led him out the door, and then he was gone without having said a word.

The office went deadly silent for about ten seconds. Then pandemonium exploded. The remaining DEA agents started gathering manila files, case files, and random pieces of paper.

I cleared my throat and read the warrant again. It was for Scot's arrest and any documents pertaining to...the distribution of narcotics? "Wait a minute." I interrupted a tug of war between the nearest agent and the receptionist over a picture of her with Stan Lee at a Comic Con. She was in her early twenties, blonde, and very chipper. Right now, she had tears in her usually sparkling brown eyes. "That's outside the scope of this warrant," I protested. No doubt any warrant. Come on.

The agent paused. He sighed, his lips turning down, as if he'd just been waiting for an argument.

I nodded. "Yeah. You've just raided an area ripe with attorneys." Yet in looking around, I was it. The only attorney on the floor. A pit dropped into my stomach, and I struggled to keep a calm facade. I'd only been a lawyer for a month. What did I know? The other attorneys were elsewhere, including my boss, who'd just been arrested.

I swallowed.

"Do something," Juliet muttered, her teeth clenched.

I blinked. "What?" There wasn't much I could do at the moment. While there should be a sense of comfort with that realization, it felt like I *should* do something.

"Anna." Clarice Jones, the head paralegal, rushed toward me with two case files in her hands. She shoved them my way.

I took them instinctively and tried to keep from falling backward. "What's going on?" If anybody knew what was up with Scot, it'd be her. They'd worked together for decades.

"I don't know." Clarice's white hair had escaped its usually too-tight bun to soften her face with tendrils. She'd gnawed away half of the red lipstick customarily blanketing her thin lips. "Worry about it later. You have to take these felony arraignment hearings. Right now."

I coughed as surprised amusement bubbled through me. "You have got to be kidding." I'd been an attorney for a month and had only covered misdemeanor plea bargains to date. Plus, my boss had just been arrested. "Get a continuance. On both of them." I tried to hand the files back.

"No." She shoved harder than I did. Her strength was impressive. "These cases are before Judge Hallenback, and he'll just dismiss if we don't show. He's not playing with a full deck lately, but he's still the judge. You have to take the hearings while Scot gets this mess figured out." She tapped the top folder, which seemed rather light in my hands. "Just follow the notes on the first page. Scot sets out a strategy for each case. The defendant will either plead guilty, in which case you ask for a sentencing hearing sometime in the next couple of weeks. Or they plead not-guilty, and you argue for bond—just read the notes."

District Court? I was so not ready for district court. I looked frantically around the mayhem surrounding me. How could I possibly go to court right now? "Where is everyone else?"

Clarice grabbed my arm and tugged me toward the door. "Frank and Alice are up in Boundary County prosecuting that timber trespass case. Melanie went into labor last night and is still pushing another one of her devil children out. Matt is with the police investigating that missing kid case. And Scot was just dragged out of here in cuffs." Reaching the doorway, which was still open, she tried to shove me through it. "That leaves you."

I dug my heels in.

The agent who'd been so determined to get his hands on the Stan Lee photo rushed my way. "You can't take documents out of here."

Relief swept me so quickly I didn't have time to feel guilty about it.

Clarice turned and glared. "These are just two case files, and the judge is waiting for the arraignment hearings." Flipping open the top one while it settled precariously in my hands, she tapped the first page with her finger. Hard. "Feel free to take a look."

Ah, darn it. The agent scrutinized the first page and then the too few other pages before looking at the second file folder. I should've protested the entire situation, but my knees froze in place. So did my brain. I really didn't want to go to district court. Finally, the agent grimaced. "All right. You can take those." He moved back to the reception area like a bull about to charge.

I leaned in toward the paralegal. "Call everyone back here.

Now." I needed somebody with a lot more legal experience than I had to deal with this.

Clarice nodded. "You got it." Then she shoved me—pretty hard —out the door. "Go to court."

The flower-scented air attacked me as I turned and strode down the steps into the nice spring day just as news vans from the adjacent city screeched to a halt in front of my building, which housed the prosecuting attorney's offices, the public defender's offices, and the DMV. The brick structure formed a horseshoe around a wide and very green park with the courthouse, police station, and county commissioner offices set perpendicular to my building. Directly across sat Timber City Community College, which stretched a far distance to the north as well. The final side held the beach and Lilac Lake.

Ducking my head, I took a sharp right, hit the end of the street, and turned for the courthouse. The building had been erected when the timber companies and the mines had been prosperous in the area and was made of deep mahogany and real marble brought in from Italy. Instead of walking downstairs like I had the last two weeks, I climbed up a floor to the district court level. It even smelled different than the lower floors. More like lemon polish and something serious. Oh yeah. Life and death and felonies. My knees wobbled, so I straightened my blue pencil skirt and did a quick check of my white blouse to make sure I hadn't pitted out.

Nope. Good. I shouldn't be too scared, because the pseudo-metropolis of Timber City had only 49,000 residents, roughly the same as a large state college. But compared to my hometown of Silverville, which was about fifty miles east through a mountain pass, this was the big city.

My wedges squeaked on the gleaming floor, and I pushed open the heavy door and made my way past the pews to the desk to the right, facing the judge's tall bench. My temples started to thrum. I remained standing at the table and set down the case files before flipping open the first one.

A commotion sounded, and two men strode in from the back, both wearing fancy gray suits. I recognized the first man, and an odd relief took me again, even though he was clearly there as the defendant's attorney and on the opposite side of the aisle as me. "Mr. O'Malley," I murmured.

He held out his hand. "Call me Chuck, Anna." He was a fishing buddy of my dad's and had been for years. "They've thrown you into District Court already?"

I shifted my feet. "It's a long story." That would be public shortly. "The DEA took Scot away in handcuffs," I said.

Chuck straightened, his gray eyebrows shooting up. "Charges?"

"The warrant said something about narcotics." We were on different sides right now, and Chuck was a phenomenal criminal defense attorney, but the truth was the truth and would be out anyway. "He probably needs a good lawyer."

"I'll check it out after this hearing." Chuck's eyes gleamed the same way they did when my Nonna Albertini brought her apple pie to a community picnic. He nodded at his client, a guy in his late twenties with a trimmed goatee and thinning hair. "This is Ralph Ceranio. He's pleading not guilty today."

Thank goodness. That just meant we would set things for trial. Chuck smiled. "Unless you agree to dismiss."

I smiled back. "I'd like to keep my job for another week." Probably. "So, no."

Chuck turned as the bailiff entered through a side door by the bench and told everyone to stand, even though we were already standing. Then Judge Hallenback swept in.

Oh my. My mouth dropped open, and I quickly snapped it shut. It was rumored the judge had been going downhill for some time, and I was thinking that for once, rumors were right. While he had to only be in his mid-sixties, maybe he had early dementia?

Today he wore a customary black robe with a charming red bow tie visible above the fold. It contrasted oddly with the bright purple hat with tassels hanging down on top of his head. A bunch of colorful drawn dots covered his left hand while a grey and white striped kitten was cradled in his right, and he hummed the anthem to *Baby Got Back* as he walked.

He set the cat down and banged his gavel, opening a manila file already on his desk. "Elk County vs Ralph Ceranio for felony counts of fraud, theft, and burglary."

I swallowed.

"My client pleads not guilty and requests a jury trial, your honor," Chuck said, concern glowing in his eyes. He and the judge had probably been friends for years, too.

"Bail?" the judge asked, yanking open his robe to reveal a Hallenback's Used Car Lot T-shirt. Oh yeah. The judge and his brother owned a couple of car dealerships in the area. If he retired now, he'd be just fine. "Hello? Prosecuting attorney talk now," he muttered.

I quickly read Scot's notes. "Two hundred thousand dollars. The defendant is a flight risk, your honor. He has access to a private plane and several vehicles."

"Everyone has a private plane. Heck. I even have one." The judge shook his head before Chuck could respond. "Fifty thousand dollars. How many days do you need for trial?"

I had no clue. I didn't even know the case.

"Probably a week, Judge," Chuck said, helping me out.

I could only nod.

"All right." The judge reached for a calendar and announced the date six months away. "See ya then."

Chuck patted my shoulder. "I'll be in touch."

I swallowed again, wanting to beg him to stay with me for the second hearing. But I had to at least act like I had a clue what I was doing. The bailiff, a brawny guy whose nightstick somehow looked thicker than usual, moved for the door he'd emerged from earlier and opened it. He grabbed an arm covered by an orange jumper while I shuffled the files and looked down, trying to read Scot's mangled notes. Hopefully I could get caught up quickly.

The judge slammed down his gavel again. "Elk County vs. Aiden Devlin for narcotics possession and intent to distribute."

I stilled. Everything inside me, from thoughts to feelings to dreams and hard reality, just halted. I slowly turned to face a tall man dressed in an orange jumpsuit. Oh my God. "Aiden," I whispered, the entire world grinding to a harsh stop.

He smiled, his eyes bluer than I remembered, his face much more rugged. "Hi, Angel."

ALSO BY & READING ORDER OF THE SERIES'

I know a lot of you like the exact reading order for a series, so here's the exact reading order as of the release of this book, although if you read most novels out of order, it's okay.

THE ANNA ALBERTINI FILES

1. Disorderly Conduct (Book 1)
2. Bailed Out (Book 2)
3. Adverse Possession (Book 3)
4. Holiday Rescue novella (Novella 3.5)
5. Santa's Subpoena (Book 4)
6. Holiday Rogue (Novella 4.5)

* * *

LAUREL SNOW SERIES

1. You Can Run (Book 1)
2. You Can't Hide (Book 2) - 2022

DEEP OPS SERIES

1. Hidden (Book 1)
2. Taken Novella (Book 1.5)
3. Fallen (Book 2)
4. Shaken (in Pivot Anthology) (2.5)
5. Broken (Book 3)
6. Driven (Book 4)
7. Unforgiven (Book 5) - June 7, 2022

REDEMPTION, WY SERIES

1. Rescue Cowboy Style (Novella in the Lone Wolf Anthology)
2. Christmas story 2022 (subscribe to newsletter)
3. Novellas 3&4 in summer 2023
4. Book # 1 launch in 2024

Dark Protectors / Realm Enforcers / 1001 Dark Nights novellas

1. Fated (Dark Protectors Book 1)
2. Claimed (Dark Protectors Book 2)
3. Tempted Novella (Dark Protectors 2.5)
4. Hunted (Dark Protectors Book 3)
5. Consumed (Dark Protectors Book 4)
6. Provoked (Dark Protectors Book 5)
7. Twisted Novella (Dark Protectors 5.5)
8. Shadowed (Dark Protectors Book 6)
9. Tamed Novella (Dark Protectors 6.5)
10. Marked (Dark Protectors Book 7)
11. Wicked Ride (Realm Enforcers 1)
12. Wicked Edge (Realm Enforcers 2)
13. Wicked Burn (Realm Enforcers 3)

14. Talen Novella (Dark Protectors 7.5)
15. Wicked Kiss (Realm Enforcers 4)
16. Wicked Bite (Realm Enforcers 5)
17. Teased (Reese -1001 DN Novella)
18. Tricked (Reese-1001 DN Novella)
19. Tangled (Reese-1001 DN Novella)
20. Vampire's Faith (Dark Protectors 8) ***A **great entry point for series, if you want to start here*****
21. Demon's Mercy (Dark Protectors 9)
22. Vengeance (Rebels 1001 DN Novella)
23. Alpha's Promise (Dark Protectors 10)
24. Hero's Haven (Dark Protectors 11)
25. Vixen (Rebels 1001 DN Novella)
26. Guardian's Grace (Dark Protectors 12)
27. Vampire (Rebels 1001 DN Novella)
28. Rebel's Karma (Dark Protectors 13)
29. Immortal's Honor (Dark Protector 14)
30. Garrett's Destiny- 2022
31. Warrior's Hope - 2023

* * *

SIN BROTHERS/BLOOD BROTHERS spinoff

1. Forgotten Sins (Sin Brothers 1)
2. Sweet Revenge (Sin Brothers 2)
3. Blind Faith (Sin Brothers 3)
4. Total Surrender (Sin Brothers 4)
5. Deadly Silence (Blood Brothers 1)
6. Lethal Lies (Blood Brothers 2)
7. Twisted Truths (Blood Brothers 3)

* * *

SCORPIUS SYNDROME SERIES

**This is technically the right timeline, but I'd always meant for the series to start with Mercury Striking.

Scorpius Syndrome/The Brigade Novellas

- 1. Scorpius Rising
- 2. Blaze Erupting
- 3. Power Surging - Winter 2021
- 4. Hunter Advancing - Winter 2021

Scorpius Syndrome NOVELS

1. Mercury Striking (Scorpius Syndrome 1)
2. Shadow Falling (Scorpius Syndrome 2)
3. Justice Ascending (Scorpius Syndrome 3)
4. Storm Gathering (Scorpius Syndrome 4)
5. Winter Igniting (Scorpius Syndrome 5)
6. Knight Awakening (Scorpius Synd. 6)

* * *

MAVERICK MONTANA SERIES

1. Against the Wall
2. Under the Covers
3. Rising Assets
4. Over the Top
5. Bundle of Books 1-3

ABOUT THE AUTHOR

New York Times and *USA Today bestselling* author Rebecca Zanetti has published more than fifty romantic-suspense and dark paranormal novels, which have been translated into several languages, with millions of copies sold world-wide. Her books have received Publisher's Weekly starred reviews, won RT Reviewer Choice awards, have been featured in Entertainment Weekly, Woman's World and Women's Day Magazines, have been included in Amazon best books of the year, and have been favorably reviewed in both the Washington Post and the New York Times Book Reviews. Rebecca has ridden in a locked Chevy trunk, has asked the unfortunate delivery guy to release her from a set of handcuffs, and has discovered the best silver mine shafts in which to bury a body...all in the name of research. Honest. Find Rebecca at: www.RebeccaZanetti.com

Made in the USA
Las Vegas, NV
03 September 2021